Marrying the Merciless Don

ASHLIE SILAS

CHAPTER 1

Enzo

Ⓞne of the first lessons I ever learned is that the world really is black and white. There are no gray areas. There's a very clear line, and the moment you cross that line, the moment your soul starts to feel a little bit black. Then, after a while, it is black, corrupted and unsavable.

I guess the gray area could be that line. The edge, the middle of black and white. But if you're already tethering that edge, you're halfway gone. You can take a step back into white, or you can wallow in the darkness.

There are good people in the world and there are bad people. And here's one thing about me you should know: Good people make me feel sick.

MY EYES SNAP open before the alarm on my phone has a chance to ring. Every day, like clockwork. Someone once asked why I bother to set an alarm in the first place, since my body is primed to wake up without it. I told him the one thing I hate is uncertainty.

I don't switch off the alarm, however, letting it continue to ring until it rouses the woman on the bed beside me. She groans, pushing her naked ass back onto my cock. I roll my eyes before climbing off the bed and crossing my arms.

"Get up," I order.

Her eyes open but her movements are slow and sluggish as she sits up. She blinks up at me, brown eyes soft, and her eyelashes flutter in a gesture I'm sure is meant to seduce. It worked last night, but it won't work again in the clear light of the day.

"Put on your clothes and leave," I tell her.

I can't remember her name. Which means she didn't tell me. If she had told me, I'd remember. All she did last night was pull me in for a kiss and ask me to fuck her. Clear, concise wording and easy access—all things I'm a sucker for. I'm not a fan of working for anything that should come easily to me, especially sex. This woman was exactly what I needed last night, considering my frustrations.

Still, when she frowns, I know I should soften my tone. "I'll have someone contact you with compensation you for your services."

When her brown eyes narrow, I know I've said the wrong thing. She flips her blonde hair over her shoulders and gets to her feet. She's a sexy woman with long legs, average-sized breasts, and full, pouty lips.

"From the rumors, I'd have thought the new Don of the Russos would have a much better bedside manner." She sniffs, moving to pick up her clothes.

I arch an eyebrow at the fact that she knows who I am. Her voice has an accent that I can't quite place. Russian, maybe? It wouldn't surprise me. The party yesterday was filled with mobsters from all over, dangerous people with ties to the mafia. I went there yesterday to scope out the people I'll ultimately have to start dealing with, but my plans were derailed by the arrival of the Christian D'Angelo. Soon, everyone was clamoring for even a second of his time.

He symbolizes everything I aspire to become. But not yet. I plan to cling to the shadows a little longer.

"My bedside manner won't be wasted on a woman I already fucked," I drawl. "But in the interest of being polite, what's your name?"

She blinks again, those long lashes fluttering before her lips stretch into a slow smile.

"You do not know who I am?" she questions. "Now, that is interesting. From the rumors, I'd have thought you knew everything."

My eyes narrow. This is the second time she's used the phrase "from the rumors."

"I know almost everything," I correct. "But no need to stroke my ego. Just tell me who's feeding you information."

Aside from the situation with the De Luca's, the mafia world shouldn't know much about me.

These past few months, I've prided myself on the anonymity. Working from the shadows is infinitely easier than working in the spotlight. And I'm slightly uncomfortable that this woman approached me knowing who I was. It means this wasn't just a casual fuck.

"You don't need to know, Enzo," she says, unsettling me even further. "But I'm sure you'll find out eventually."

She finally finishes dressing, pulling on the dress she wore last night.

"And when I do?" I challenge.

She smiles. "Then I'll come find you. Or not. It depends

on the next moves you make. Who you choose to ally your-self with."

"What the fuck does that mean?" I ask calmly.

"You'll understand soon, Enzo," she says, still vague, sliding into her heels before rising to her feet. "For what it's worth, I had fun last night. Don't insult me by having someone contact me for any sort of payment. I am not a whore, Enzo. Goodbye."

She blows me a kiss before walking out of the hotel room. Once she's gone, I get dressed, jaw clenched as I try to figure out the interaction and the conversation. If there's one thing I hate, it's feeling out of control. And she's right. I also despise not knowing things.

Once I leave the hotel, I head to my car and driving toward the Russo mansion, a place that feels less like home every time I step into it—despite it being the only home I've known all my life. There are a few nods and salutes from the men guarding the place as I walk in. I open the giant double doors and catch the ball flying toward my head seconds before it can make contact. An eyebrow lifts as I study the ball in my hand, and my eyes trail over to the direction it came from.

The kid gasps and his blue eyes widen as he takes a step back in fear.

"For fuck's sake," I mutter.

I walk over to Matthew Russo. He has short, curly brown hair, chubby cheeks and a cute smile. At least, I guess his smile is cute, but I wouldn't know because he hasn't smiled at me since he met me a few months ago. Not that I blame him. His father died and I showed up to take his place.

I force my expression to be neutral as I get on one knee in front of the seven-year-old, handing him the ball. He accepts it with shaky fingers.

"Hey, bud," I say. "Were you planning on hitting my face with that?"

He shakes his head and swallows softly. "No, *cugino* Enzo."

"Alright. Cause if you were, you're a terrible shot. It's okay to want to hit me in the face, but if you're going to do it, you should do it right."

He tilts his head in confusion, and I sigh.

"We've talked about this, Matthew. You don't have to be scared of me. I'm your cousin. Family. We protect each other. And sometimes, we feel like beating each other up. But that's okay."

"That would sound so much better if you didn't kill his father six months ago," a voice pipes up.

Rolling my eyes, I let out another sigh and get to my feet. My gaze immediately connects with Isabella Russo's icy blue eyes.

"Hello, *cugina mia*. How's your day going?" I say with false enthusiasm. "And could you not say stuff like that in front of the kid?"

"Why not?" Isa shrugs. "He knows the truth."

She gestures for Matthew to come over and he immediately does, moving to hide behind the cousin he trusts. I can't blame them for their attitude toward me, but there comes a certain point where you've got to give a guy some leeway.

"I didn't kill his father," I state.

Isa tilts her head to the side, expression cold. "No, you just had someone else do your dirty work. *codardo*," she spits, calling me a coward.

My jaw clenches. I have a lot of self-control, but these past few months, Isabella has gotten pretty good at pushing my buttons.

A tense silence follows as I stare at her, but it's quickly

broken when Jason strolls into the living room. He takes in the atmosphere with a raised eyebrow.

"Could we have one normal morning in this house without it feeling like World War III's about to break out?"

"Shut up, Jason," Isabella snaps before walking away, taking the kid with her.

I watch them go, wondering when I'll be able to fix my relationship with my cousins. Or if I even should. Despite what they may think, I've got nothing against them. I came back for my family. And they're a part of that. I'm here to protect them, whether they realize that or not.

"You, come with me," I say to the insufferable blonde.

Jason follows me up the stairs to the office on the second floor. It used to be a library, but I had it converted into my office. I refuse to use the same office that my father and his brothers made use of in this house. I can barely even set foot in it. Jason takes a seat opposite me as I tell him about the woman I met last night.

"Pull up the footage from the party last night and find her. I want to know everything. Her name, where she's from, hell, even her credit score."

Jason scratches the scruff of his beard. "You sure that wouldn't be a waste of resources? I mean, you've got more important shit to do than think about a chick you already slept with."

I give him a hard look. "She said something about me being careful who I choose to ally myself with. In what world is that not something I have to look into?"

"In a world where you're not a control freak," he mutters, and my eyes narrow.

Jason's the only person apart from my cousins who is allowed to speak to me that way. I've known him for a long time, ever since I left home and went to London. One night, I was out late after having too much to drink, and I stumbled on this thin, wiry English kid with blond hair and hollow cheeks. He was able to steal my wallet and my phone, which was already impressive. What he didn't know was that I'm pretty good at tracking things that belong to me.

I found him and held him at gunpoint, but instead of begging for his life, he smirked at me and told me to make it a kill shot. He was the kind of fearless you don't see every day, so I decided to keep him around. He's become the person closest to me in the world. He's an idiot, but he's an irreplaceable one. I wouldn't be where I am now without Jason.

"Don't make me repeat myself."

"Alright, I got it," he says on a sigh. "I'll find your girl. Have you heard back from De Luca?"

I nod. "Roman has agreed to a meeting. He's suspicious as hell, which is frankly annoying considering I saved his daughter's life."

"After your uncle jeopardized it in the first place. And you did use her as a bargaining chip."

"Good point," I murmur. "At least now I've got something else to bargain with."

"Let's hope he bites."

"He will," I state, completely assured.

Jason leaves, and the rest of my day is spent trying to fix my family's crumbling empire, while adding last minute touches to my plan to ensure it goes off without a hitch.

Unfortunately, even the most foolproof plans can end up blowing up in a person's face. People can be fickle. And while I can control most eventualities, I have no control over a person's mind or actions.

I'm sure Roman will be easy to convince. His sister, though, that's a whole other issue.

CHAPTER 2
Rosa

In royal families, when two kids are born in line to inherit the throne, they are sometimes referred to as the heir and the spare. I can relate to that. I've related to it my whole life. While my family's not royalty, we're pretty damn close.

Roman was the heir and I was the spare. And I've always been content with that. I was the family's little girl, and I got pretty much everything I wanted. I was allowed to stay as far away from my family's business as possible, which suited me perfectly. My brother lived his life doing away with whatever humanity he had; meanwhile, I grew up with as much of my humanity as possible.

With a family like mine, it's incredibly easy to lose yourself. But I've always known exactly who I am. And I've always known what I want. The only problem is, it's not always easy to get those things. Especially not when you're the princess of a mafia family in the Cosa Nostra.

So, while a major benefit is that I was able to retain most of my humanity, the downside is that I've never had any freedom. My mother taught me that freedom is a luxury I can't afford. But she also taught me that there are various ways to feel free. And one such way is through art. When I'm sculpting, painting, drawing, those are the only times I ever truly feel in control.

My heels clack against the marble floors until I stop in front of a large canvas. Something inside me stirs. If you know what to look for, you can tell exactly how an artist was feeling when they created their work. I stare at the depiction of the burning house and the sun above it that seems to be the reason for the destruction. If you look closely, the sun almost has a face—almost.

"That looks nice," someone says from behind me. "Is it yours?"

The voice is entirely unfamiliar, and unwelcome. Very slowly, I turn around. And oddly enough, my heart skips a beat. I'm not particularly sure why. He's wearing a navy-blue suit with crisp lines and a perfectly knotted tie. A chill caresses my forearms as his gaze trails over my face.

His light blue eyes are crystal clear, like glass. He has short, full, reddish-brown hair. It looks soft, soft enough to run my hands through. But I can't think about that, especially when something about him reminds me of my brother. Dangerous, powerful. And definitely not good for me. There's an air of superiority around him, an arrogance carved into him. He's about six feet tall, which is tall, much taller than me. But he's still not as tall as some of the men that surround me every day. And yet the arrogance around his posture and aura makes him seem much bigger, larger than life. I swallow softly.

It takes a few seconds for me to remember he asked a question.

"No, it's not," I say, hating how breathless my voice sounds.

He smiles. It's a soft one, but I can tell it's not genuine. And that more than anything else jolts me back to reality.

"Wait. Why would you think it was mine?" I ask curiously. I'm just a woman walking around an art gallery. How would he know I was an artist? "Do you know who I am?"

"Smart girl," he says, placing a hand in his left pocket. He looks slightly impressed.

I frown. "Who are you?"

"I could tell you," he says, cocking his head to the side, "but I don't particularly want to."

I arch an eyebrow. "Why not?"

"Because," he drawls, "I simply don't want to."

Forget his handsome face. I'm not sure I like him or his attitude.

"Okay then," I say dismissively, turning back to the painting.

Still I feel his presence behind me. His stare prickles the back of my neck. I'm all too aware of him.

"What do you feel when you look at it?" he asks softly, not leaving. "Come on, you can at least answer that."

His tone is cajoling, making me want to reveal all my secrets.

"It's unsettling," I mutter. "But also brilliant, alive. The artist seems a little narcissistic, but it's a vivid painting. It tells a story that calls to people. Even if it's not the same story everyone can see."

"And what story are you seeing right now?"

His voice is smooth like velvet, wrapping around me like a caress. Enticing me to reveal my secrets.

"I think it's sad," I say, my gaze drifting to the man in the painting, dying alone on the horizon. The sun burns, the house burns, and he dies. "You can lose everything in the blink of the eye. The world takes and takes until there's nothing left to give."

"There's always something more to give," he says from behind me. "Even in death, we all still have souls."

I smile softly. "Not everyone's soul is redeemable. Not everyone has a soul left to give."

"Hmm," he says, making a noise I translate to be agreement. "It was nice to meet you. I'll see you again, Rosa."

I'm so focused on the painting it takes a few seconds to realize he called me by my name. By the time I turn around to question him, he's gone. I catch the sight of his broad shoulders as he turns, disappearing behind the hallway leading out of the building.

I'm still staring in the direction when Daniella D'Angelo approaches. She's the owner of the gallery, and one of my friends. She takes in my expression with a frown.

"What's wrong?"

I'm extremely unsettled. "Did you see the man that was talking to me?"

"Well, I saw the side of his face. It looked like a really good-looking face," she says with a smile.

"And you didn't recognize him?"

She shakes her head. "No, did he say something?"

"Not exactly. But he knew who I was. And he didn't tell me who he was."

This feels like the kind of thing I should mention to Roman. But if I tell my brother, he'll probably blow things out of proportion. Ever since his daughter was kidnapped, he's been anal about security and safety. It took weeks before I could convince him to let me leave the house without a constant shadow. And I'm still not sure he agreed. Knowing Roman, he probably got me a shadow that's great at blending in.

"If you're this upset, we could find him. Christian connected a facial recognition software to the CCTV. I'm sure we could get a hit."

I consider saying yes, then decide against it. I'm a De Luca. There are tons of people in New York who know who I am. If it's not due to my family, it's due to my art. Him knowing my name doesn't mean he means me any harm. I don't like that he alluded to us meeting again, but really, no harm was done.

"No, it's okay. I'm just overreacting. I'm sure it's nothing."

"Are you sure?" Daniella questions, green eyes shining with concern.

"Yes, I'm fine," I reply with a smile. I lean forward and hug her. "Thank you. You're a good friend."

"I know," she agrees, making me laugh.

Having nothing left to do, I leave the building and head home. As soon as I step through the doors, there's a little baby waddling toward me. I immediately drop to the ground and pull her into my arms. Cassiopeia De Luca will be one year old in a month. She's growing up so fast. I feel like I blinked and she was crawling. Then walking. And now she's even talking.

"*Zia*," she says with an adorable smile, babbling some other words.

"Hello, my darling," I say, planting kisses on her cheeks.

Holding her in my arms, I rise back to my feet. My eyes meet the eyes of her mother, who's staring at us with a bright smile.

"Hey, Lena," I greet, walking over to her.

"Hey, how was your day?"

We head into the living room and take a seat on the couch. I tell her about going to the art gallery and a new deal

I might be getting with a company looking to purchase some pottery pieces. I don't tell her about the strange man who approached me. Lena and I have known each other for a long time, since we were kids. But she's my brother's fiancée, and while I trust her, there's a possibility she could tell him.

"So, where's everyone?" I ask, pinching Cassie's cheeks.

She giggles and my heart melts. I love her so freaking much. Seeing Cassie makes me wish for kids of my own. But not yet.

"Roman and the guys are out doing whatever it is they usually do. I texted him a few minutes ago and he told me they'll be home soon. Oh, and I talked to Maria and my dad. They'll be back in time for Cassie's birthday."

"That's nice," I say.

My mom went on a trip to Milan a couple of weeks ago, and I kind of miss her. When she's here, she tries to dictate every aspect of my life from what I wear to the way I speak. But mothers do that, I guess. And while our relationship has some bumps, she's also my rock. Plus, she's the only parent I have left.

Elena's telling me about the party that she's planning for Cassie's birthday. It took a lot of convincing to get Roman to have a party in the first place. His major problem was that it's a security risk, Then there's the fact that we're planning their wedding as well.

My eyes trail down to the diamond on her finger. It's simple, yet elegant. And honestly it's so perfect. It took a lot for her and Roman to get to the point where he was getting down on one knee and asking for her hand in marriage. But they got there. And they're amazing together.

"We should have a theme for the party," Elena states. "Cassie loves playing with her pink doll. I was thinking we have a pink party. Everyone wears pink, the decorations are pink."

That makes me grin. Elena and her crazy ideas.

"I'm not saying I hate it, Lena. But can you imagine my brother wearing a pink suit? How would you even get him into it?"

"I'll convince him," she says, waving a hand nonchalantly.

"You won't," Roman retorts, tone resolute as he walks into the room.

He drops onto the couch beside Elena. Tony appears at my side next, wrapping an arm around my neck and cutting off some of my air circulation.

"Ow, dude!" I say, slapping his arm away.

He chuckles, reaching for the baby in my lap, and grabs her before I can protest. I glare at him and let out a huff of irritation. Tony might be Elena's older brother, but it's almost like he's mine as well. I grew up with three insufferable ones. I'm sure the last one came home with them, but Michael's so anti-social and quiet, he doesn't like spending time with people unless he has to.

"I kind of like the idea of a pink party," Tony muses, letting Cassie squeeze a finger in her fist. He looks up at us and grins. "Chicks dig guys in pink, right?"

I make a face. "Ugh, you're disgusting."

"You mean amazing, Rosy. Amazing."

"Why does a party even have to have a theme?" Roman asks, sounding exasperated.

We both turn to the couple arguing quietly. Elena's sitting next to him with one leg on his thigh, and her eyes have that stubborn look in them. Unfortunately, that look is also mirrored in my brother's eyes.

"Because it does. Don't argue with me, babe."

"I already agreed to this party, *lupacchiotta*. A pink theme sounds excessive. And I have a feeling you'll decide on something that'll drive me crazy. Like a masquerade."

Elena makes a face like that's not a bad idea and Roman groans, head falling back. I laugh. He can make all the complaints he wants, but I know he'll do whatever she asks.

"What were you up to, anyway?" Elena asks him. "You said you'd be back early."

For a minute, I think he'll evade the question. Especially if it has something to do with death or illegal activities. I'm used to him being vague about what his business entails. But to my surprise, he answers.

"We were preparing for a meeting with someone. It's in a week."

"Who?" I immediately ask.

"The new Don of the Russos. He's asked for an audience," my brother says.

"Why do you look so worried?" Elena questions.

Tony speaks up. "Because the guy's fucking crazy."

"Crazy good or crazy bad?" I ask.

Tony pauses, thinking about the question.

"We don't know," my brother says. "We don't know anything about him, actually. He's the one who returned Cassie to us when she was kidnapped. He became the Don after that incident and since then has been conducting his business low-key. We don't have much information on him."

"He's a slippery eel," Tony mutters.

"At first glance, he's just as dangerous as the next made man in the Cosa Nostra. But he hasn't been in the Cosa Nostra all these years. The guy showed up a couple of months ago, had his uncle killed, and then claimed the title of Don."

"And now he's asking for a meeting?" Elena asks.

"Yeah. I told him it would be on our own turf. He can

only bring a man or two. I'm curious to hear what he has to say."

Elena arches an eyebrow. "You like him."

My brother's eyes narrow. "No, I don't."

"Please, you were talking him up just now. You're at least intrigued by him," his fiancée teases.

"I'm curious," he corrects. "He seems like my kind of person, though."

"A caveman with no sense of humor and control issues?" I interject with a smile.

His gaze cuts to me with a glare. "Very funny, *sorella*."

I shrug.

"Just be careful, okay?" Elena asks, drawing his eyes back to hers. "Your new best friend could very well want a fight."

"Nah, I doubt it," Roman says. "He's not an idiot."

"You just said he was crazy," I mutter.

"He is," Tony states. "But you can be crazy and smart."

"That barely makes any sense."

He sighs. "Trust me, Rosy, we know."

"I hate that we know next to nothing about him," Roman says. "But he asked for an audience, and we're going to hear him out. Enzo Russo has no choice but to be careful. Right now, he's trying to piece back his family's reputation. He won't do anything dumb."

Enzo Russo. I turn the name over in my head. I have to agree with my brother. He actually does sound interesting.

CHAPTER 3

Enzo

W e're searched three times before we're allowed in the private offices of the Don of the De Lucas. By the time the door opens, I'm feeling slightly irritated, and my lips curl into a smirk as I take Roman in. He's in a black suit, seated behind the desk with a calm, controlled expression.

"You know, if you were worried I was carrying a bomb, all you had to do was ask," I say, walking into the room.

Jason's right behind me. I take in the other occupants of the room. Roman's cousin Michael is standing behind his chair. Tony's against the wall, cool brown eyes revealing his annoyance.

"You carrying a bomb?" Roman asks with a smirk of his own.

"Nah. If I was, we'd all be blown up by now," I tell him, taking a seat in front of him without being told to.

Jason stands beside the closed door, arms crossed over his chest. Roman's blue eyes flick over to him inquisitively.

"That's my best friend, Jason," I inform him. "He's kind

of like my Tony or Michael. Except he's not as unhinged as Tony or as good with computers as Mikey over there."

"Hey," Tony speaks up, affronted.

Mikey's expression only flickers while Roman's jaw clenches.

"You've done your research," he says with a short nod.

"Of course. I make a point to get to know my business partners," I tell him, leaning backward in my chair.

I undo a button on my suit, letting it fall open. I'm the picture of ease, something I'm sure will annoy Roman.

"Business partners?" he asks an edge to his voice.

"Yes. As soon as we can come to an agreement."

"You keep talking about agreements and deals. But I've never given you any inclinations that I'd like to enter into one with you. I don't know you; I don't like you," he states.

"That's really mean, Rome. You know much more about me than most people," I state. "For example, you know my name. You know my face. I'd say that's plenty information."

"I also know how it feels to want to put a bullet in your skull," Roman tosses out.

"Woah," I chuckle, "easy with the threats. We haven't even gotten to the good stuff."

He tilts his head to the side and shrugs. "Alright, fine. What do you want, Russo? And it better be worth my time."

I lean forward. "Like I've been saying since the first time we spoke, Roman, I want a partnership. You and me, we've got the potential to do something really amazing here. You've just got to be open-minded. I want you to not only see the big picture, but imagine it in your mind."

"Get to the point."

I pause, scratching an eyebrow before saying the words, "A marriage alliance. Between our two families."

Roman stiffens. In my periphery, I see Tony's eyes widen. Michael's the only one who doesn't seem to react.

"What the fuck are you talking about?"

He wasn't expecting this. But he could have at least given it some thought. Turned it over in his mind. I inwardly sigh.

"Alright, listen. There are currently four powerful mafia families in New York. After you obliterated the Gallos, no one has come up to take their place. It leaves the Russos, the D'Angelos, the De Lucas, and the Mincettis. We're the top dogs. Now, imagine how great it would be if the two top dogs had an alliance," I explain. "I'm aware you already have a close friendship with the D'Angelos, but the Don and his two brothers already have wives. It makes sense for you to align yourself with us."

Roman's eyes are darker than ever. But he manages to get a word out.

"And the Mincettis?" he asks.

Very subtly, I grit my teeth. "We both know they're not partnership material."

Except when they send their daughter to sleep with me and get information.

It was fucking hard to find out who the blonde was. And it was even harder for me to decide what to do with what she said. But at the end of the day, I decided to go with my gut. The Mincettis are unpredictable. There's not a lot I know about them. And despite their offer of an alliance, I'm going with the De Lucas. Better the devil you know.

Roman could have killed me when he thought I kidnapped his kid, but he didn't. I admire that. I may have killed him if I thought he was involved with my kid's disappearance, Or maybe he somehow knew I didn't have anything to do with it.

I came back home and found the kid just laying there in

the dark. I was pissed off that my uncle kidnapped a fucking child. I told him he needed to make things right or the De Luca's would have his head but he lost control. He wanted to be a hard-ass and it cost him his life.

I know my cousins would never understand and would have preferred I waged a war against the De Luca's but they already had my uncle and getting him back would have costs us more men. He made a decision to be a dumbass and I wasn't about to endanger the rest of our family for his poor decisions. In fact, it made it all clearer that I needed to take my place as the don.

I stare at him intensely awaiting his response. Roman's jaw practically grinds. "You want a marriage alliance," he says slowly. "Marriage with who?"

I smile. "Me, of course. Last I checked, Rosario De Luca's perfectly single."

"You fucking bastard!" Tony yells.

Almost immediately, all hell breaks loose. Tony rushes at me, but I'm out of my chair in seconds. Before Jason can move forward, I have Tony's arm behind his back and his face on the table. Roman gets to his feet, his gun out and pointed at me. Michael does, too. I don't hesitate to grab the knife in the hidden pocket of my suit.

Tony lets out a slew of colorful words.

"Well... this escalated quickly," I mutter, placing my knife against the pressure point of his neck. I look behind me at Jason, who hasn't moved an inch. "Feel like contributing?"

He shakes his head and gives me a thumbs up. "You got it, boss."

I roll my eyes, looking back at Roman. "Come on, let's put the toys down."

He looks furious. There's even a tiny vein bulging on the side of his forehead. "You first."

"I didn't attack first, now did I?" I retort.

Roman looks at me, then at his brother who's still struggling against me. Tony's strong, but I've got several pounds of muscle on him.

"Fine," Roman bites out, dropping his gun.

Michael follows suit. I remove my knife from Tony's neck and move backward. He glares at me, but one look at Roman has him inching back to the wall.

"Now, can we have a civilized conversation?" I ask.

"Alright," Roman replies, pulling back his chair and lowering down into it. "Have a seat."

"No thanks," I say with a small smile.

Roman smiles, too. He links his hands together and rests his chin on them. When his eyes meet mine, I know he has regained some semblance of control.

"Now tell me, why the hell would I let my sister marry you? In case you didn't realize, your family's the one in a life boat. The De Lucas are thriving. We don't need you."

I cock my head to the side. "Except that's a lie. Isn't it?"

Roman's eyes flare. "What?"

"You lost your biggest source of funding when you broke your word and refused to marry Zanetti's daughter. That's a huge deal—one you've been trying hard to hide these past few months. You have a problem. Am I wrong?"

A muscle ticks in Roman's jaw. "You know, you're a fucking asshole, Russo."

"No. I just know everything. And it's pissing you off," I state with a shrug. "Now, do you want to hear what I've got to offer in exchange for Rosa's hand in marriage and an alliance between our families?"

"I'm not giving you my sister," he grits out.

"Oh, come on. Families around here do it all the time. Take, for example, your bestie, Christian D'Angelo. He was in an arranged marriage with his wife, wasn't he? And you were supposed to be in an arranged marriage with the Zanetti girl. Before you broke it, of course," I say. "In our world, it's pretty normal."

"I don't give a fuck about normal. I'm not marrying my sister off to a fucking psychopath."

I sigh. "Roman, you're being really dramatic."

Surprisingly, Michael speaks up. "What do you even have to offer? You keep talking about offering something in exchange. What is it?"

I give him a smile, glad to see someone's priorities are in line with mine. Michael frowns back, his expression distasteful. I wave him over, and Jason places a file in my hand. I set it on the table in front of Roman and, after a second thought, return to my previous seat.

"I have money. Lots of it," I say with flourish. "Money you currently need. Managing all those drug fields in different countries must be taking a toll on you. I heard Zanetti's blocking your contacts at the border, keeping your stuff from coming into the country. I can fix that for you as well. If there's one thing the Russos are good at, it's underground work. My uncles might have been idiots, but they did well to maintain my father's connections."

Roman's gaze flicks up from the contract at that. He leans backward in his chair, eyes inquisitive.

"Let's set the contract aside for a moment. I want you to tell me about you, Russo. You show up in town out of nowhere, and we can't find any information on you. Who the hell are you? And your father?"

I crack my knuckles, holding his stare. A part of me understands his request. It's annoying, though.

"My father was the Don of the Russos about twenty years ago." I say, scratching my jaw, pretending there's not a tiny lump in my throat. "He was murdered one extremely cold night in our family home. My mother was killed, as well. I was ten years old, and I had to watch it happen. Fun times."

The room grows eerily silent. Roman's expression is unreadable, but when I look at Michael, I see some sympathy directed at me. It would piss me off, except I understand it's not pity. I know Michael's story. He lost his parents young, as well.

Roman clears his throat. "That's fucking tragic, man."

For some reason, that makes me laugh. "It's alright. They died, and Uncle Miguel became Don. He was awful at it, but he managed to keep it together for a time. Then he grew older, sloppier. I'm sure you're aware that he died about two years ago. Then Leo became Don, which was around the time I started preparing to return. Leo was an even bigger idiot than Miguel. Anyway, you know the rest of the story. And how I got here."

"That's vague as hell," Roman states. "Where have you been the past twenty years?"

"Oh, you know, here and there. I lived in the U.S. till I was eighteen, then I left. Visited a couple of countries. I even picked up Jase over there in one of them," I say, gesturing behind me.

Roman's gaze doesn't let up.

"Look, where I've been is irrelevant. What matters is that I'm here now, and I'm proposing a deal. Look it over. You and I both have important things to do. But you're in big trouble right now and I need your help, as well."

The words "I need help" feel like ash in my mouth. I haven't wanted or needed any help since I was a kid. Not since I needed help saving my parents, yet... no one came until it was too late. But desperate times call for desperate measures. And the Russos will never amount to anything if I don't secure our title. I made a vow to rebuild my father's legacy, and that's exactly what I plan to do.

"Alright," Roman says. "I'll look over the contract. That is not a yes."

"But it's a maybe," I state, unable to keep the triumph from my voice.

"Hmm. It's a pretty big maybe. I'm not keen on marrying my sister off to a man I barely know. And there's no way I could convince my family to agree."

"I'm sure you'll figure it out. You might not know what my word is worth yet, but I swear I'll take care of your sister. If you agreed to a match, I'd treat Rosa like a queen. She deserves it."

He arches an eyebrow. "You sound like you know her."

I smile, getting to my feet and redoing the button in the middle of my jacket. "Like I keep telling you, I know everything," I say cockily.

Roman's unimpressed. "Stay the fuck away from my sister, Russo."

Unfortunately for him, I don't do well with being told what to do.

"Let me know when you're ready to review the contract," I tell him. "And I can promise you that if you agree, I'll take it a hell of a lot more seriously than you took the contract with the Zanettis."

His eyes narrow. "Fuck you, Enzo."

I chuckle. "See you around, Roman."

After one last look at Tony and Michael, I leave, feeling slightly accomplished. Jason trails behind me all the way to the car. He only relaxes when we're handed our weapons. Three guns and two knives for him, which is overkill. I accept the weight of my gun into my palm and slide it into the back of my pants.

"So," he drawls as he drives us away, "that went well."

I shrug. "It went as well as it could have."

"You think they'll agree?"

"He doesn't have any other choice," I mutter.

"But you do."

I think about the blonde Russian with her sugar-coated words and vague promises.

"No, I don't. The Mincettis are dangerous. I'm not inviting people like that into my bed."

"You already had one in your bed," Jason retorts.

"Drop it, Jase. The only woman I want in my bed now is Rosario De Luca."

He chuckles and lets out a small whistle. "Damn, I can't imagine you being monogamous, E. That'll be a sight to see. You're going to marry this chick without even knowing her?"

"We wouldn't get married immediately," I murmur.

I don't mention that I already met Rosa or the fact that she intrigues me. When I first heard about the De Luca princess, I expected a mild-mannered woman who would lie down unmoving while she was fucked. But she's got a fire in her. One I wasn't expecting. One that makes my blood heat. It doesn't help that she's fucking gorgeous. The thought of her silky straight black hair and stunning blue eyes has me clenching my jaw.

Not everyone has a soul left to give.

Truer words have never been spoken, although I do find it odd that she said something like that. My future bride is much more jaded than I expected. Which is interesting.

I have a habit of getting bored fast. But I have a feeling that's not going to happen with Rosa.

CHAPTER 4

Rosa

S omething's wrong. My eyes collide with Elena's over the tense silence at the table as we eat dinner. It's been like this the past two days. And I keep waiting for them to tell us what it is, but all three of the guys have been silent.

It has something to do with the meeting with this Enzo Russo guy, but my brother is being incredibly tight-lipped about it. He didn't even tell Elena and she's beyond pissed. Even baby Cassie is starting to be affected by the atmosphere.

A fork clangs against a plate as Elena rises to her feet.

"I can't do this anymore," she mutters, reaching for the baby in the high chair beside her. "If you all insist on continuing to act like someone's dead or about to die, then I'm not spending any time with you."

With that little announcement, she walks out of the dining room. Roman drops his fork as well and leans back in his seat.

"You've got to tell her, man," Tony speaks up from behind me.

"Yeah, I will," he murmurs, running a hand through his hair.

"Um, excuse me," I say, raising a hand. "I'd like to know, too."

"Not you," Roman says with a scowl.

My eyebrows rise. "Hey, don't bite my head off."

He groans. "You're right. I'm sorry, *sorella*."

"Whatever the Don of the Russos said must have really rubbed you the wrong way," I muse. "So what is it, are you guys going to war again? Are we safe?"

"We're safe," Michael assures me. "And we'll fill you in later, Rosa. We're just trying to take care of some issues."

I really don't like the troubled expression on Roman's face. He's always so confident, on top of his game. I want to push and force them to tell me what's wrong, but that's not a battle I can win.

"I'm putting you back under security detail, by the way," my brother states. "You don't leave this house without at least one guard."

"What? No way," I immediately protest. "I don't need a bodyguard."

"Trust us, Rosy," Tony says gently.

My hands clench into fists. "Is this about Russo? You just said you weren't going to war."

"We're not," Roman replies.

"Then why the hell are you suddenly being particular about my safety?"

"Because you're my sister."

"Try again."

Michael sighs. "Rosa, it's for your own good. It's not that we believe you're in any danger. We're just taking precautions."

"If I'm not in danger, why do you have to take precautions?"

No one replies. I let out an exasperated huff before getting to my feet and leaving the room. Sometimes, I really hate the family I was born into. My feet move toward my art studio of their own accord.

I inhale the clean, earthy scent of the room, letting it calm my senses. It's comforting. My studio is messy, which is to be expected. There's a tarp covering the floor in the area of the room that has my wheel, some tools, clay, and a kiln to the side. I glide over and take a seat, staring at the piece I was working on.

Usually when I try to sculpt something, there's an image in my head, something I'm trying to bring to life. But these days, I've been feeling empty. Maybe empty's not the right word. More like bored. I've also tried painting, and while it's not my strong suit, it's helped me in the past. Every single time I picked up a paintbrush, though, I've had this mental block.

I don't create art for money. It's not a job, more of a hobby. I sometimes sell my work, but I don't do so often, which means there's no pressure to create something new. I can take things slow. No pressure means no heartache. I usually can't create art unless I'm in a bad place emotionally. Eventually, I'll find my groove again.

For now, I just have to be content with the sense of calm being in this room provides me.

I SLURP the milkshake in front of me and let out a soft sigh of contentment. Food really is one of life's most underrated pleasures. I could be having a horrible day and the one thing that's bound to cheer me up is a good meal. Or sweets. I notoriously have a sweet tooth. Chocolates and candies are my weakness. I'm grateful every day for my metabolism, which helps me stay somewhat fit and in shape.

Kiara, who's seated in front of me, doesn't seem to share my sentiment with regard to the cup of deliciousness in front of her. She twirls it absentmindedly. It isn't until I reach for her cup to gain her attention that her head snaps up.

"Hey, milkshake thief. You have yours right in front of you," she says.

I laugh. "Welcome back. What's up with you? Is everything okay?"

"Everything's fine. I guess." Then she leans closer and lowers her voice. "Is it just me or are you also feeling extra single now that Lena's getting married?"

"Not really," I say carefully. "My last relationship ended badly. I'm trying to squeeze in as much me-time as I can. I'm not really keen on another one."

Kiara crosses her arms over her chest and her brown eyes soften, "You're right. But I just feel... lonely, I guess. It doesn't help that I live alone since Lena and Cassie moved out."

"If it's too hard, you could always move into our house. There's plenty of room," I suggest.

"And live with Michael? No thanks."

It intrigues me that that's her biggest problem.

"Why not? Aren't you two still best friends?"

"Not like we used to be," Kiara states. "We hooked up and he asked for some space afterwards. Typical Michael fashion, he took several steps backward. Intimacy's hard for him. He doesn't connect well with people. And I try so hard to be patient, but I can't wait for him my entire life."

My heart aches for her. And for my cousin. I don't blame

him for how he turned out. He's so strong, and I admire how far he has come.

"Just don't give up on him, okay?' I say softly.

She smiles and offers me a small nod. We go back to slurping our milkshakes, but suddenly, Kiara's tilting her head to the side, her black hair falling over the side of her face.

"Rosa... don't look now, but there's a guy behind you who keeps staring at our table."

I do the complete opposite of what she said and immediately turn around, eliciting a groan from Kiara. When my eyes find a pair of familiar blue ones, I almost choke on air.

"Oh, shit," I say, whirling around. "What the fuck?"

Kiara raises an eyebrow. "Do you know who that is?"

"Not exactly," I mutter.

"Hm. He's insanely hot," she muses. "Like really, really good-looking."

"Would you quit staring at him?" I snap.

Kiara does something insane and waves instead. My mouth falls open.

"What?" she asks when she notices my expression. "He waved first."

I rub my hands over my face and groan. "Yeah, that's it," I say, getting to my feet.

Her expression grows worried. "Where are you going?"

"I need to speak to him. Just wait here, okay?"

She nods and I turn around, heading for his table. He doesn't look the least bit surprised as he watches me approach.

Damn, he looks good.

It's not something I should be noticing, but Kiara's right. At first glance, he looks like a gentleman, like he belongs in a board room. But if you really stare at him, the discrepancies come into focus. The dangerous edge in the relaxed set of his shoulders, the shadows beneath his eyes. His brown hair is messy, which is odd considering his general put-togetherness. It looks just-fucked in a way that, in another life, would have me drooling. In this life, it just irks me that he's exactly my type.

I slide into the seat in front of him.

"Hey, beautiful. You know you really shouldn't approach strangers in restaurants?" he questions.

"And you really shouldn't be stalking people," I retort.

"If you think I'm a stalker then why did you come over here?"

"Maybe I just like to live dangerously."

"I doubt that," he says, blue eyes steady. "But you're drawn to me, aren't you? Curious."

I scoff. "No, I'm not. Not really."

"So you don't want to know who I am?"

"I already know who you are, Enzo Russo," I say casually. I make sure to look him straight in the eye.

His expression doesn't so much as flicker, but his mouth does curve into a small smirk. And just like that, I know I'm right.

"How?" he asks, confirming it.

"Lucky guess." I shrug. "It wasn't that hard; my brother suddenly becomes serious about security the moment you show up making demands he's having trouble dealing with."

"What do you know about my demands?" Enzo asks.

"Nothing. Should I care about them?"

He's amused. "Maybe, maybe not."

"Vague," I mutter, irritated that they're all being so secretive.

"Don't worry, *principessa*. It'll all make sense soon enough."

"And you're going to stop stalking me? Your good looks

aren't going to keep me from going to my brother about your behavior."

"You won't tell him," Enzo says confidently.

"You think?"

"Yeah. Because if you told him, he'd be furious. He would try to make me stop, and I'd have to fight him."

"So you're saying you would fight him if he told you to stop seeking me out?" I ask, confused. "Why?"

He doesn't reply. But his eyes do flare slightly with heat.

"Don't worry, Rosa. Like I told you, it'll make sense soon enough," he says, getting to his feet. His eyes move to where Kiara's still seated. "Why don't you head back to your friend?"

"Why don't you stop stalking me!" I retort.

He smiles in amusement. "I'm not stalking you, Rosa. I was here first." he says as the waiter returns his card and the receipt from his bill.

I get to my feet as well and cross my arms over my chest. When Enzo takes a step forward, my heart speeds up. I have to incline my head slightly to look him in the eye. I feel an unmistakable urge to look away, but I don't. I'm not wearing heels today, just black flats.

"Whatever game you're playing with my brother, I don't want any part of it," I tell him, my voice firm.

This time when Enzo smiles, it's a sort of sad smile. He lifts his hand to my cheek and brushes it softly. Goosebumps spread across my skin at his touch, but I have enough sense to inch away and glare.

"I'll see you again, *principessa*," he says softly.

And then he's walking away. I stare at his back for a few seconds before turning around and heading back to Kiara. As soon as I slide back into my seat, her mouth opens.

"Don't ask," I immediately say, stopping her.

Her mouth clamps shut, but she frowns. "Everyone has a phase where they're interested in the bad boys with smoldering hot looks. But I swear that man feels dangerous, Rosa. It's his aura or something."

"I know he's dangerous," I mutter.

"Then you know you have to be careful."

"I'm not interested in him," I say defensively. "He just keeps showing up."

"Then tell your brother."

"No." I shake my head. "That would be like adding petrol to a fire."

Kiara sighs. "Alright, then I guess I'll just sit back and enjoy the show."

I want to tell her there's no show. But my head spins as I try to make sense of all that I've learned. It's pretty clear now that whatever's going on between the De Lucas and the Russos has something to do with me. But I can't figure it out.

What do you want with me, Enzo Russo?

———

THE TRUTH DOESN'T ALWAYS SET you free. I learn that a week after my meeting with Enzo in the restaurant, when my brother walks into my bedroom and explains to me that he needs my help. My mother raised me to be compliant. A good Italian girl does whatever it is that's asked of her, especially when it's for the good of our family. Women are there to keep the house from burning down. According to Roman, our house is on fire.

And I'm the only one who can save it. The only problem is, to do that, I have to marry a stranger.

A stranger with light blue eyes and a painfully handsome face. A stranger I'm pretty sure could be the devil in disguise.

My throat is dry but I manage to find the words. "You're asking me to get married to a man I barely know?" I ask my brother, unable to keep the betrayal from my voice.

An arranged marriage was always in the cards, but a part of me thought that with my father dead and my brother a bit more understanding than our dad ever was, I would be able to avoid it. But it's pretty clear now that there was never any avoiding it. This was practically written in the stars from the moment I was born.

Good Italian girls do as they're told and marry who they're asked to marry. Like a lamb to fucking slaughter.

CHAPTER 5

Enzo

I n wars, the most respected generals are the ones who
know when it's time to call it quits. To sound the alarm
of retreat. Those people are intelligent enough to pick
the battles that will ultimately help them to victory. I'm glad
Roman is one of such people.

His jaw is tight as he signs the documents that effectively
seal his sister's fate while also ensuring our partnership. It's
pretty clear he's not happy about it. But being in charge
means making hard decisions.

Once we're done affixing our signatures, I get to my feet
and stretch my hand for a shake, which he grudgingly
accepts.

"I look forward to a fruitful alliance," I tell him.

"Yeah, yeah," he mutters. "Hurt my sister and you'll
regret it for the rest of your life. Which I guarantee will be
painfully short."

The threat is delivered in a cool, assured tone. I smirk.

"I'll take care of Rosa."

He nods, blowing out a breath and running a hand
through his hair. We're the only ones in here. Roman's left-

and right-hand men are nowhere to be found, and Jase is waiting for me back in the car. I study him for a few seconds.

"Any reason you're this wrought out?"

His gaze meets mine sharply. "Apart from the fact that I feel like I'm selling my sister?"

"That's stupid. She's not cattle to be bought or sold."

"Said by the man who's quite literally buying her," Roman says dryly.

"Does she think that? That she's being sold? I imagine you told her about the arrangement and got her permission before signing the contract. How does she feel about it?"

Roman pauses. "I wouldn't know. She hasn't spoken to me in a week. Not since I told her about it. She agreed, but I can tell it hurt her to do so. She's been avoiding me, and I'm not sure I'm ready to face her either."

Sympathy swirls within me. For him. While I care about my family, I'm extremely removed from their feelings and emotions. I barely know them. Isabella and I might have grown up together, but my leaving as a teenager signaled the end of any form of relationship we built. I wasn't around for the birth of the twins. So, while we may call ourselves family, there's no inherent bond.

Roman doesn't have that luxury. He can't afford to be callous about their feelings because he loves them, which further solidifies what I've always known. That love is a weakness. Or perhaps a luxury I can't afford.

"I'm sure she'll come to terms with her situation soon enough. Especially since she'll have to move in with me later this week," I state. It was one of the conditions I expressed upon completion of the deal.

Roman's dark gaze cuts sharply to mine. I arch an eyebrow at the expression on his face.

"I haven't told her about that yet," he informs me. "I'll leave that task to you. She's your future wife, after all."

"Hmm. And when do you suppose I tell her?"

"My daughter's birthday is tomorrow. You're invited. It will give you a chance to meet the family, and you can talk to Rosa as well."

I nod. "Alright. Then I guess I'll see you tomorrow."

THE DE LUCA home is a large mansion, secluded in a neighborhood that grants them privacy and a sense of safety. It's eerily similar to the Russo home. The house is simple, understated, with smooth walls and modern furniture. There's a lot of art around the house, mostly sculptures and clay figures. I'm drawn to them, pieces I'm sure were made by Rosa. It's amazing that her hands can create things as intricately pretty as the vase in front of me. It's inside a show glass with a few other similar ones lining the walls. There are paintings mounted, as well. Some bear her signature, others I guess must be purchases.

Her love for art is a clear difference between us. I've never much cared for it or tried to understand it. But she seems to do so, deeply. I'm still staring when I feel a presence behind me. I turn slowly to find none other than Elena Legan, soon to be De Luca. She doesn't even try to mask her dislike for me. It shines in the flare of her green eyes.

"Hello," I say.

"Save the pleasantries," she tells me, holding a hand up. Her gaze trails from my face to my outfit—a three-piece black suit. "You were aware of the dress code, were you not, *cognato*?"

Her tone is hard as she refers to me as her brother-in-law.

I shrug. Roman did inform me that it was an all-white party. I take in her white dress with a small smile. "I don't wear white. It's bad for my reputation, *cognata.*"

It's cute that we're already calling ourselves such familial names when I'm not even part of the family yet.

"And what reputation would that be? Because, frustratingly enough, no one seems to know much about you. And you're going to be marrying one of my best friends."

"You'll find out about me in due time, Elena," I assure her. "In the meantime, I'd like to get to know my future wife."

She scoffs. "Good luck with that. Rosa might be kind with the biggest heart ever, but even she isn't okay with being sold into marriage."

"Take it up with your fiancé, not me," I mutter.

"I have. But there are some things that are out of my control," she says sadly. "If you hurt her, I'll—"

"I've heard enough threats, thank you," I say, cutting her off.

She frowns. "I really don't like you."

"Things change."

She rolls her eyes and walks away, toward the back of the house where the party's being hosted. I should follow her, but for some reason, my legs stay in place in front of the sculpted pieces. A few seconds later, I'm rewarded when I hear footsteps descending the steps.

I turn and Rosa appears. Something inside me sinks at the sight of her. She really is beautiful. Like a rose. She was aptly named. Beautiful and fragile. I'd hate to break her, but I'm not sure I know how not to. Her dark hair flows past her shoulders and she's wearing a white dress that stops at her mid-thigh. It's simple, understated, and yet the way it hugs every single one of her curves is a sight to behold.

I've always liked a little weight on women. Rosa's body is full in ways that make me itch to hold her. Her gaze is fixed on her phone as she steps down, high heels clacking against the surface of the shiny light brown steps. She's almost at the bottom when her head finally lifts and her eyes collide with mine.

She sucks in a breath and her blue eyes widen. For a moment, we just stare at each other. And then her eyes narrow and she turns around. I immediately move, climbing the stairs. My arms close around her wrist before she can go back up. I tug gently.

"Hey," I say.

She turns, albeit begrudgingly. "What do you want?"

I smile, amused. "That's hardly the way to talk to your future husband."

Her gaze sharpens and she rips her hand away. "Listen, I already agreed to marry you. But that doesn't mean I'm ready to be subjected to any time in your presence right now. I'm still coming to terms with all this. So, if you could leave me alone?"

I pretend to think about it for a moment, placing a finger against my chin. "Rosa, I…" I begin, trying to find the right words.

Her eyes flutter shut and her hand goes up to her forehead, massaging it gently. "Why did you even ask for me? Why do you want to marry me?"

"It's not about marrying you, per se. Don't get me wrong, you're a beautiful woman, but I would have married anybody to guarantee the stability of my family. I needed you, Rosa. It's as simple as that. Do with that information what you will."

Although, I would have married Rosa for nothing. There really is a fire in her that draws me in.

She pauses, letting that sink in. "That's honest of you."

"You'll come to realize this in time, but I don't lie."

She scoffs. "What? Never?"

I shake my head. Lying signifies a fear that someone can use whatever you say against you. To hurt you, whether intentionally or not. I don't have such a fear.

Rosa seems to consider this for a moment. "So if I asked you something, no matter what it was, you'd answer me honestly?"

"*If* I answer, then yes, you can be sure it's honest," I state.

She nods in understanding. "Okay. So why did you approach me? Before."

"I was trying to gauge your reaction to me. Our natural chemistry," I reply with a smirk.

She rolls her eyes. "I'm guessing you were sorely disappointed?"

"Actually, you seemed to like my good looks, so…" I trail off.

Her eyes widen. "What? I didn't!"

"You did, *principessa*. I distinctly remember you saying something about my good looks."

She huffs out a breath of irritation and looks away. I chuckle.

"You know for our first official conversation, I'd say we're doing alright," I tell her.

"You'd say," she mutters.

I place a hand on her shoulder, trying to coax her into looking at me. "Come on, we can have a fresh start." I stretch my hand toward her for a shake. "I'll go first. Nice to meet you, I'm Enzo Russo."

She stares down at my hand for several seconds, then her gaze goes up to my face. Her lips thin in distaste. "A part of me wants to shake your hand and start this relationship amicably. But then I remember you were involved in Cassie's kidnapping."

I inwardly groan. "Like I've said a million fucking times at this point, I saved that little girl. You literally owe her life to me."

"Just because you did one good thing doesn't mean you're not a monster," Rosa says, voice hard. "I-I wanted better for myself."

My jaw tightens. I take it back—this is going terribly.

"We can do this the easy way, or the hard way, Rosa."

Her blue eyes narrow, like she's more than ready for a fight.

"I choose the hard way."

"Okay then," I say. I take a step forward, shifting closer to her. She standing one step above me, but my height allows us to be eye level. "I was going to ease you into this information, but since you're going to be difficult, pack your bags. You're moving into my house before the end of the week."

I hate that the look of horror on her face fills me with some sense of vindication.

CHAPTER 6
Rosa

I officially hate my future husband. Which is unfortunate, because the husband part is something I have no control over.

He trails behind me as I storm toward the back of the house. The festivities are underway, with the majority of the guests seated at the long table. Elena's seated at the head of the table with Cassie in her arms. My niece seems to be loving all the attention, and I'm glad for it. She deserves to have the best birthday, even if she won't remember it in the years to come.

My eyes roam the area until I find my brother. He's standing away from the party, having a discussion with Tony. His eyebrow flicks up when he notices me approaching. His gaze hardens, and I know he must notice Enzo behind me.

"You told him I could move into his house before the end of the week?" I hiss.

He frowns. "Calm down, *sorella*."

"Don't tell me to calm down! I'm not an object, Roman. You can't just dangle me around like a puppet. I would do anything for our family, but at least think about my feelings."

I love my brother, I really do, but sometimes I really hate what he's become. What our world forced him to become. He's a great big brother, caring, a little overprotective, but I can understand that. Although we didn't grow up particularly close, that has more to do with our upbringing. And in the past few years, ever since our dad died, I thought we were bridging the gap. But I can feel our bond fraying with this decision. I want to understand it, but I can't. Especially not right now.

"Rosa, you're going to get married to him. When he made the request, I thought it was ridiculous but it makes sense. You need to get to know each other. You need to meet his family and acclimate to his life."

"I'll do that at my own pace. Not because you or him command it," I say harshly.

Roman opens his mouth to speak but clamps it shut when our mother approaches. There's a frown on her face, caution directed at us in her eyes. We're still in public, after all. My gaze moves to the table filled with the party guests, who keep glancing over here. I force myself to remain calm.

My mother stops in front of Enzo, and I turn to watch as she regards him with a cool gaze. Enzo straightens his tie and clears his throat.

"It's a pleasure to meet you, ma'am," he tells her.

"It would have been nice to meet you before I consented to your marriage to my daughter."

My jaw clenches. It would have been nice if she had employed that tone when Roman first told her about the match. Instead, she decided to trust that he knew what he was doing.

"Of course," Enzo says with a charming smile. "That was my mistake. Rest assured you'll be seeing much more of me from now on, Mrs. De Luca."

He's perfectly polite, poised. I practically see my mother thawing. It makes me sick. While Enzo continues to impress her with his wiles, my brother places his arm around my shoulder and leads me farther away.

"Rosa, I know this is hard," he starts. "And you have every right to be upset. I'm not fond of this, either. But I need you to trust me on this."

"This doesn't have anything to do with trust," I state.

"No, it doesn't. Tell me, *sorella*, what are you so afraid of?"

I open my mouth to speak, then shut it as I ponder his question. "Everything," I say, finally deciding on the answer.

Roman nods, his dark blue eyes shining in understanding. "I get it, and it's perfectly okay to feel that way," he says. "There's something else I need to tell you. Another of Enzo's terms is that the marriage happens before the end of the year."

My stomach roils. That's in less than seven months.

"I know," Roman says, taking in the expression on his face. "It's fucked up. But it's also why I didn't fight his request to have you move in so soon."

My brother places a hand on my shoulder. I look up at him and his gaze is hard, unflinching.

"You're my sister, Rosa. My family. I would never put you in harm's way. You have a few months to spend some time with the guy, so get to know him. And if he hurts you, or hell, if you feel you really can't get married to him, just let me know, okay? I'll break the contract without a second thought. I'll get you away from him. I swear."

His words warm my heart. And I didn't realize it was exactly what I needed to hear.

"You promise?"

"I promise, *sorella*."

He stretches his pinkie out toward me, the gesture

reminding me of the times he would do something bad when we were kids and make me promise not to tell.

He pulls me into a short hug and presses his forehead against mine.

"*La famiglia al primo posto. La famiglia sempre.*"

"Family first. Family always," I whisper back in English.

He nods and we both turn around to find more than a couple of eyes on us. There's an intense look in Enzo's eyes when mine meet his. My heart jolts.

"I don't know if I can love him, Rome," I say softly.

"Love is never easily achievable," my brother says. "All you can do is keep an open mind and try, Rosa. He might not be the monster you think he is."

Oh, God, I really hope not.

THE DAY I'm scheduled to move into my future husband's home, he doesn't come to pick me up. Instead, I find myself face to face with a blond man with steely gray eyes. He's good-looking, but the scar on the side of his face makes his beauty seem cruel, harsh. His arms are crossed as he leans against a sleek blue Jaguar. I stare at him curiously.

"Who are you?"

He smirks. "Pleasure to meet you, Mrs. Russo," he says, tipping an imaginary hat at me. He has a faint British accent. "I'm Jason Reid. Your driver."

"Please don't call me that. And I don't need a driver."

"Oh? Then that's good because I'm not one," he says dryly. "I'm actually Enzo's best mate. But don't tell him I said that. He likes to deny the fact that he loves me so much."

I stare at him for several seconds, trying to figure out the man in front of me. Finally, I sigh. Of course, Enzo's best friend's personality is just as weird as his.

"He sent you here?"

"Yeah. Asked me to deliver his bride-to-be in a perfectly wrapped parcel." His gaze flicks to the suitcase I'm holding onto. "Is that all your stuff?"

"I'll come back for the rest later," I inform him.

He shrugs, grabbing it and placing it in the trunk. I turn back to look at the house I've lived in since I was born. A sense of melancholy fills me. I already said my goodbyes earlier at breakfast. The mood was dour a little depressing. Elena was pissed. My brother and the guys tried to be more upbeat, encouraging, but I could tell they aren't too excited that I'll be gone. My mother didn't show up. I talked to her last night, and while she agrees with the wedding, she's not happy that I'll be living with him so soon.

I got so angry at her. Of all the things to be mad about. She didn't care that I was entering a marriage with a man I didn't know—all she was worried was how it would look to everyone. I hate that I'm leaving while we're in a fight, but it's not like I'm going far. If my mom wants to talk to me and maybe apologize, she can pick up the phone and do so. Or ask someone to bring her to me.

"Need a few more minutes?" Jason asks from behind me. His tone is slightly teasing.

I roll my eyes. "No, let's go."

The drive is mostly quiet. Jason strikes me as a guy that doesn't talk much but notices plenty. I guess he can tell I'm dreading this. Leaving my home, moving into a new one. I'm terrified by the uncertainty. I have no idea what I'm walking into.

Thirty minutes later, thanks to New York traffic, we're pulling into a fancy neighborhood. I'm surprised the Russos live in a place like this. There are a lot of people on the sidewalks; I notice a grill out and a small party on someone's lawn. Compared to my quieter, much more private neighborhood, this place seems so much more outlandish. Right in the heart of things, populated.

For a mafia family, I'm not so sure that's advisable.

"We own most of the houses on the street," Jason says, interrupting my thoughts.

I jerk slightly, turning to him. "What?"

"The reason the neighborhood's so crowded. I know you were wondering," he says with a small smile. "We own the houses. Apparently, Enzo's dad liked to dabble in real estate, so he bought every house on this street to ensure his family had privacy. But after what happened last year, Enzo decided that might not be the best idea."

I arch an eyebrow. "What happened last year?"

"Well, your brother barged in and practically kidnapped a Don, then killed him. The men were taken off guard. Most of them were spread out across the city. The Don decided that had to change. Since he took over, loyalty to the Russos has meant getting a roof over your head."

"That's... ostentatious," I mutter.

"Go big or go home." Jason shrugs.

He pulls up in front of a huge, shiny black gate, and after a few seconds, they swing open automatically. He drives up the driveway until we're parked in front of a large mansion. Not that different from my home, except it feels colder somehow.

"Come on, I'll show you around," Jason says, pulling out my suitcase and moving to stand beside me.

"Where's Enzo?" I ask, my voice coming out sharp.

Because, really, he's the only person I kind of know. And he should be here right now.

"No idea. He's probably inside," Jason replies.

I let him lead me into the mansion. He's showing me to the living room when someone appears in front of us. Icy blue eyes eerily similar to Enzo's narrow onto me.

"And you are?" she asks, tone bored.

Beside me, Jason smiles, amused. "You know who she is, Isa."

Isabella Russo. Enzo's cousin. I'm glad Roman didn't let me come here blind. He coached me on what to expect from Enzo's family. He has three cousins, and Isabella's the oldest. Then there's the twins. Two kids who are about seven years old. The last family member in the house is Enzo's aunt, the wife of the former Don. The one my brother killed. He warned me to stay away from her if I could.

"Even if you don't, it's nice to meet you, Isabella. I'm Rosa," I say, trying for a warm smile.

Isabella glares at me in response. She reminds me of the bitchy girls in high school who liked to think they were above everyone and everything.

"Just stay out of my way and we won't have a problem," she says with a snarl before promptly walking away.

"Well, that was nice."

"She'll come around eventually," Jason offers. "I promise she's not always so bad."

"I'll have to take your word for it," I mutter. "Could you please take me to Enzo? I need to talk to him."

He considers my request and shrugs. "He's probably in the gym room. Go up the stairs and take a left. It's two black double doors, you can't miss it. I'll take this up to your room for you."

I nod, "Thank you."

"You don't have to thank me."

Jason leaves and I find my way to the location he described. I'm struck by how impersonal the house feels. There aren't any pictures on the walls, no paintings. The dark paint only adds to it all. For a house that's been lived in for probably as long as mine, it feels very cold. It kind of reminds me of Enzo himself.

Thankfully, I find the gym without running into anyone else. I push the doors open and immediately come to a stop. Enzo's in the middle of the room, face screwed up in concentration as he lifts two large weights that if I had to guess must be double the size of my body mass. That's not what makes me pause, though.

He's shirtless. Sweat clings to his chest and his muscles ripple and contort as he lifts the weight. It's inherently sexy. My mouth dries and I swallow. He hasn't noticed me yet, which is great because it would be mortifying if he saw me caught off guard like that. I realize he doesn't know I'm here because his ears are plugged. I move closer until I'm standing over him. His eyes widen slightly in surprise. A tiny part of me had been hoping to surprise him enough to drop the weights, but of course, that doesn't happen.

Not that I wanted him crushed. Not really…

His mouth stretches into a smile as he maintains his grip on the weights. I step back so he can lift them back in place. He moves with ease after that, sitting up on the bench. He takes the earbuds out and looks at me. Instead of meeting his eyes, my gaze trails down his body. To the very prominent scar on his chest. It's the only imperfection on his body—a faded scar running down from his sternum to just above his stomach.

"Hi, honey," he greets enthusiastically.

"What happened there?" I ask, pointing at the scar, because while it might have been a little rude to ask Jason about his scar, I don't have any qualms with regard to my future husband.

Enzo's jaw tightens. "That's on a need-to-know basis, Rosa," he says, getting to his feet. "And you don't need to know."

I incline my head to look him in the eye. "Ten seconds. That's how long it took before you started keeping things from me."

When he smirks, it feels dangerous, cutting.

"You really thought I was just going to be tell you every-thing? That's cute, *principessa.* Real cute."

My hands curl into fists. I made a decision to at least try to make things work. Because while my brother might have made me a promise, it wouldn't be fair to put him in such a position. I had hoped Enzo wouldn't be such an obscure person. Maybe if he showed me something real, I could find a way to understand him. But it's clear he has no plans to do so.

Which means we're quite literally at a stalemate.

CHAPTER 7

Enzo

I tilt my head to the side, staring at her. Every conversation we have can't end in a fight. That would be redundant and terribly unhelpful. I sigh, heading for the towel I left on the table. I clean off the perspiration gathered on my chest before turning to assess my future wife.

Her expression is tight and her jaw is set in a way that's a little adorable. It's pretty clear she's going to continue being difficult. Which is unfortunate. I was a fool to think this would be easy. It's not like I can force her into submission.

"How did you enjoy the drive here?" I ask, trying to change the subject.

To my surprise, she relaxes slightly. Her expression clears.

"It was fine. Jason was nice. He didn't talk much."

"Yeah, he tends not to with people he's unfamiliar with," I say. "He's a dumbass, though. You'll like him once you get to know him."

"Okay, good, because your cousin hates me."

I wince. I don't have to ask which cousin she's referring to.

"Can't help you with that one, sorry. She hates me, too."

"Why?"

I shrug. "There are a lot of reasons. If I'm being honest, none of my family members particularly like me."

She arches an eyebrow. "Good to know."

"Don't worry, I'm sure you'll charm them in no time. The twins will like you."

"The kids don't like you either?"

"Well," I drawl, "I did have their father killed. It's been hard to breach that gap."

"Oh, right," Rosa says under her breath. "And my brother was the one that actually killed him. I guess I'm fucked."

That makes me chuckle. "Don't worry, I talked to them and they won't hold it against you. It might take them a while to open up, but they will. Maria even smiled at me today. And she called my name. Which is progress."

"Okay," Rosa nods. "So… what now?"

"I'm not done with my workout," I inform her. "You could join me if you want. Maybe run on the treadmill. It's a great way to release tension."

Her lips purse. "I don't run unless someone's chasing me. Or if it's for charity."

Charity? Oh, my sweet little rose.

"I can believe that," I say as my lips twitch. "So what do you do for fun, *principessa*? Besides pottery and art and charity, apparently. We might as well start getting to know each other."

"Right now, I'd like to rest. I didn't sleep well last night. So if you could just throw on a shirt and show me to the bedroom I'll be using, that would be much appreciated," she says pointedly.

I consider it for a moment before shrugging. "Come on, then," I say, leading her out of the gym.

Her heels clack against the floors as she follows me downstairs. There's a long narrow hallway and I stop in front of the last door, opening it and gesturing for her to walk in.

"Your bedroom, my lady," I say with mock flourish.

While she takes it in, I head into the closet and grab a shirt to wear. When I return, Rosa's still looking around wide-eyed.

"Enzo," she starts, "why does it look like you sleep in here as well?"

"Because I do," I reply easily. "It's my bedroom."

Realization flickers across her blue eyes, followed by subtle horror. "You want me to sleep in the same bed as you."

"We are going to be married," I point out.

"In *months*," she hisses. "We're going to be married in months."

I watch as she moves toward the dark brown suitcase at the edge of the bed. She grips the handle as she stares me down.

"I'm not staying here with you," she says, her voice hard.

"I'm not sure why this bothers you so much."

"Are you kidding me? Enzo, you want us to sleep in the same bed! Together."

"Which is typically what married couples do."

"We're not married yet!" she practically screams. "And I'm not doing it. Either give me my own bed in separate room or I'm leaving."

The threat leaves her mouth on a whisper, and something inside me chills once she's said it. I move toward her, my steps light but intentional. She freezes, alarm tainting her features. A hard smile slashes across my mouth.

"Let's go over the ground rules, shall we, *principessa*?" I ask. "First one, threaten me with that again and I'll make you regret it. You're mine. The minute I signed that contract with your brother, you became mine. I won't tolerate you saying shit like that. Okay?"

She sucks in a breath. The sweet scent of apples fills my nostrils at our proximity. My hand goes up to her wrist, and I can feel her pulse racing as I gently run my finger over it. It's a light touch, but from the way she's looking at me, one would think I was trying to hurt her.

"What are you planning to do with me?" she asks in a whisper.

I withdraw my hand, my eyes meeting those fierce blue ones. "I guess that depends on how well you behave. I gave you a chance to start this amicably and you threw it away. I know you don't know me very well, but I pride myself on being reasonable, rational. I entered this match because I felt it was the smart thing to do. I don't like being wrong. Are you going to prove me wrong, sweetheart?"

She swallows softly and my gaze is drawn to her throat. So… delectable. And distracting. Very slowly, she shakes her head.

"Good. I like that we're on the same page," I say with a small smile. "I realize you don't like me much, and that's okay. In public, we'll play the role of a loving couple. I understand you're very immersed in society. We'll attend a few events together, smile for the cameras and pretend."

"I thought you said you didn't lie," she whispers.

This close to her, I can take in every inch of her flawless skin. Long dark lashes frame her deep blue eyes, and the curve of her lush lips is just as distracting as the rest of her. Heat spreads from my gut to my stomach at the sight.

"That's not a lie, Rosa. We're just going to be putting on a great show," I tell her, taking a step back. "If you walk out, you'll find a door right before this room. That door leads to your bedroom."

She takes in that announcement with a clenched jaw. "You're a fucking bastard."

"You could always sleep here, if you'd like. I wouldn't mind the company," I say "And before you go off about me lying, I never specifically said you would be sleeping in here."

She appears to ponder that for a moment. "That's your thing, isn't it? Finding loopholes. Bending the rules."

"I do have a special talent for it. It's been very important to my survival."

"Being an asshole has been important to your survival?" she tosses out.

"No," I grin, "that's just a nice perk."

"You can go. Dinner's at seven. Feel free to do whatever it is you'd like until then."

"Oh thank you, your majesty," she says sarcastically. Her hand tightens on the handle of her suitcase.

She moves to walk out but then pauses. "Enzo?"

"Hmm," I reply.

I decide that I like the sound of my name on her lips.

"Have you ever thought that the reason your family hates you so much is because you don't have a heart?"

"The thought plagues my every waking moment," I say sarcastically with a mocking smile.

Inquisitive blue eyes trail over my face. I grit my teeth at her perusal.

"You know, I actually thought I would hate you, but the truth is, I don't. At least, not really. I feel sad for you. The loneliness, the isolation from your family, that scar on your chest. I've only been here for a few minutes and I can already see the cracks. You're quite pitiful, aren't you?"

I don't lose my composure very often. I do everything with control. But once in a while, something comes along that makes me slip. And when I slip, it's never good for the parties present.

Rosa only has time to let out a small squeak as I advance on her. I have her flat on her back on the bed in a matter of seconds. This time when my hand closes over her neck, the touch is anything but gentle. I squeeze. It's not hard enough to bruise, but it's just enough to feel the shallowness of her breaths.

My voice drops dangerously low. "I don't need your fucking pity, Rosa. This is a business arrangement. Nothing more, nothing less. If you're going to be a bitch, we might as well just ignore each other. I don't give a damn either way. Is that what you want? For me to stay away?"

She continues to stay silent, so I press a thumb against her pulse. Hard.

"Answer me," I grit out.

Her eyes flash. "Yes. I want you to leave me alone."

"Fine," I say through a clenched jaw.

I climb off the bed and take a step back. Rosa's eyes briefly flutter shut before she stands, as well. The look in her eyes is mutinous.

"I'll stay away. But I expect you to be a good little wife. Understand?"

Her lips press into a stubborn line, but I know she gets it. She continues to glare at me as she grabs her suitcase and storms out of the room.

"See you at dinner, sweetheart," I call out after her.

"Fuck you!" she shouts without looking back.

I'm actually quite amused that she's still bold enough to swear at me after that but she is a De Luca. I need a shower. Especially since having her pinned under me has effectively made me hard.

I blow out a soft breath, suddenly hating the way I acted. Control.

A few words and it slipped from my grasp. Rosa De Luca might be a little dangerous, after all.

CHAPTER 8

Rosa

A s far as I'm concerned, my entrenchment into the Russo house goes seamlessly, I think it has more to do with the fact that almost everyone is intent on ignoring me. We all eat together, breakfast and dinner. Enzo sits at the head of the table. I sit on his right, Jason on his left. Isabella sits beside the twins. And we all do our best to ignore each other. The only person who really talks is Jason. And while he does his best to pull us into conversation, it's pretty clear no one's interested.

Enzo's still angry. On some level, I can understand my contribution to the way he acted. I pushed him until he lashed out. That's on me. And I hate that I couldn't keep my promise to myself to at least try to make things work but it's not like I can do it alone. I'd like for him to make a real fucking effort as well.

A week passes by where I only see him at meals. He doesn't even look at me. We're nothing more than house-mates at this point. At least Isabella makes sure to acknowl-edge me with a glare or a snide word or two. Enzo stays silent. He's doing as I asked, but it's really starting to piss me off.

We're having breakfast when I clear my throat to draw his attention. His eyes flick over to me, as do everyone else's at the table.

"Yes, Rosa?" he asks, tone perfectly pliant, light.

"I'd like to leave the house today. A friend of mine invited me to an auction and showcase."

Enzo thinks about it for a moment before nodding. "Okay. Jason will go with you."

"Actually, you asked me to oversee something on Long Island today, remember?" Jase asks.

"Right," Enzo mutters.

"You can go with her if you're worried," his friend presses.

A sharp glare has him immediately clamping his mouth shut. My lips twitch when he even goes so far as to mime shutting it with a padlock and throwing away the key. He really is a dumbass. He kind of reminds me of Tony, and my heart aches at the thought of my family back home. It's only been three weeks, but I miss them. Sure, they all call, but it's not the same. At least I know I'll see Elena at the auction today, since she was also invited.

"I'll have a guard escort you," Enzo announces.

I'm surprised when a small feminine voice speaks up. "What type of showcase is it?"

Maria is an adorable child with chubby cheeks, light brown eyes, and long black hair. She's also much more forthcoming than her brother, who is incredibly shy. Sometimes I'm not sure if the kids don't like me or if they're just uncomfortable with a stranger. I'm leaning more toward the former, however, considering they treat their cousin more or less the same. The only person they're really comfortable with is Isabella. And sometimes maybe Jase.

"It's an art showcase, *cara*. I'll get to see different paintings and sculpting's and artworks," I say warmly, glad she's finally speaking to me.

Her brown eyes alight with interest. "Are you a painter? My mama says I'm a good painter."

Her elusive mama, whom I have yet to see since moving into the house. She mostly stays locked in her room. The only people she sees to are her kids, and Enzo seems content to leave it that way.

"I'm sure you do. And yes, I do paint," I tell her. "But I'm more into pottery."

"Pottery?" she questions.

Her twin is completely silent beside her, more focused on his food than the conversation happening around him.

"Yes. It's sculpting with clay. Don't worry, I'll show you sometime," I assure her. "Or you could come with me today, if you want? I'm sure you'd love it."

Maria thinks about it for a second. I watch as her eyes trail to Isabella, whose expression is blank. Then she looks at Enzo. Finally, she sinks back in her chair and shakes her head.

"No, I'll stay here. Thank you."

I smile. It's not like I can force her. And she has impeccable manners. "It's okay."

Breakfast continue silently, and after we're done, everyone disperses. It's a weekend so the twins don't have school. They follow Isabella, who seems to love having them around. It's clear she adores her little cousins.

After Enzo and Jason leave to conduct their business for the day, I head back into my bedroom which is fast becoming my sanctuary in this house. The only thing I hate is its proximity to Enzo's room. I hear him come in sometimes at odd hours of the night. I've toyed with the idea of approaching him and forcing a conversation but managed to convince myself otherwise every single time.

There's a man waiting to escort me when I arrive outside of the house. He offers me a short nod and opens the back door of the car for me. Once I'm inside, he gets into the driver's seat and starts the car. An hour later, I'm among a group of friends, sipping champagne and trying my best to forget just what a mess my life is right now.

"We haven't seen you around much," one of my friends says, nudging me with her shoulder. I met her at an exhibit a few years ago. We're acquaintances, always running in the same circles. "What's going on? Get a new boyfriend?"

I still. Enzo made it clear that I wasn't to tell anyone aside from family about our arrangement until he's ready to go public with it. Thankfully, Elena, who's also standing in the circle saves me.

"Actually, we've been busy with wedding preparations. That's why Rosa hasn't been around much," she lies smoothly.

That seems to appease the women in the circle. Except Daniella.

"So, no boyfriend?" she presses curiously.

I smile and shake my head. "Nope."

"That's a relief," someone says from behind me.

I turn and find myself face to face with a man I don't recognize. He's Asian, with dark brown eyes and short brown hair, a perfectly carved jawline, and a small smile on his face.

"I'm sorry, do I know you?" I ask.

His expression grows wounded. "You don't know who I am? You pain me, Rosa, truly."

I look back at the circle for someone to provide an explanation.

"He's Alexander Wong," Daniella informs me.

"The guy everyone is talking about these days?" I ask dryly.

Apparently, he's Picasso come back to life. I've seen some of his art, but I hadn't met him. Until today.

"I'm glad to see you do know of me," Alexander says from behind me.

I turn back to him. "Yes. How may I help you?"

"You could help me by going on a date with me," he states, getting straight to the point.

My jaw threatens to drop but I manage to school my shock. The women behind me make sounds of surprise and delight, clearly impressed.

"I'm flattered," I say softly. "But no thank you."

His expression flickers. I get the feeling he's not used to being turned down.

"That was harsh," he murmurs. "You didn't even think about it."

Because I can't. I shrug and offer him an apologetic smile.

He sighs. "Okay, then. I'll leave you to your friends."

He leaves and I turn back to the excited women who immediately pounce, talking about how romantic that was and how I should have said yes. I catch slight worry flickering in Elena's eyes, but she masks it and offers me a small smile. I'm eventually able to escape the ladies to peruse some of the paintings on my own.

"That's one of mine," a voice says from behind me.

A sense of déjà vu hits me. His appearance is reminiscent of Enzo's the first time we met at Daniella's gallery. I sigh softly but don't turn around. My eyes stay fixed on the painting.

"It's beautiful, isn't it?" Alexander asks.

"Would be nicer if you weren't so cocky," I mutter.

He chuckles. "Alright, I'll tone it down. But seriously, tell me what you think. You're an extremely talented artist. I would value your input."

After a second's hesitation, I decide to oblige.

"It's inspiring to see how you capture emotions and create a visual narrative through your work. The composition is well-balanced, and it's clear you paid particular attention to detail. Your use of light and shadow adds depth to your work. My only complaint is that it seems a little dark."

Alexander moves beside me. He's much taller than me; I barely reach his shoulders.

"You and I both know that the darkness is what really draws people in," he states.

Tell me about it. He and Enzo would be great friends.

"Not everyone's a fan of darkness."

"Well, in that case, you and I are perfectly suited. I'm all light, beautiful. I can show you just how light over dinner tomorrow."

My lips twitch but I hide the smile. "Can't take a hint?"

"Unfortunately, I'm incredibly tenacious. Meaning you're stuck with me until you agree to the date," he says with a bright smile. "Unless there's a reason you can't."

"There is. I'm not interested," I deadpan.

"Come on. You're hot, I'm hot. You're an artist, and I'm one, too. We already have loads in common. And there's chemistry. There's literally nothing stopping us."

The last time a guy thought we had chemistry, I ended up in an arranged marriage with him. Still, I don't think Alexander's someone I need to be worried about. And like he said, he really is hot. If he had approached me a month ago, I might have taken him up on his offer. But it's too late now.

I look up at him, meeting his eyes.

"I really am sorry. You're definitely interesting. But my answer is still no."

He sighs. "Not even if I say pretty please? I'm gonna be honest; I've watched you for months, Rosa. Trying to work up the nerve to talk to you and now that I can you're shutting me down. You're really hurting me here."

I'm a little touched by his words. And a little disappointed. If he had approached me months ago, maybe we would both be in completely different places.

"I'm sorry," I say again, for the lack of anything better to say.

He shrugs. "It's alright. But you won't mind if I escort you for the rest of the evening? You could help me find my next purchase at the auction. We could dissect art pieces that aren't mine, maybe make fun of them," he suggests, playfully waggling his eyebrows.

"Actually, we already have plans," Enzo's voice reaches me from behind. I turn around, and there he stands. Captivating, exuding confidence and power.

With a single rose in hand, he stands tall, his magnetic presence commanding attention. His chiseled features and self-assured demeanor create an aura of undeniable allure.

"Enzo, what are you doing here?" I ask, still slightly taken aback.

"I was hoping that maybe we could check out some pieces together. You know I don't really understand any of this crap, so it'd be senseless to walk without you. What do you say?" he asks.

I laugh. "Alright, fine. I'm in." I offer an apology to Alexander and walk away with Enzo.

"Is this rose for me, or are you thinking of giving it to

someone else tonight?" I gesture towards the flower he's holding. His eyes lock onto mine, a mischievous spark igniting between us. "To someone else? Never," he whispers, the hint of a smirk playing on his lips as he sensually places the rose in my hair.

For an electrifying moment, he lingers, our gazes intensifying. The air thickens with desire, and my breath hitches as the magnetic pull between us becomes undeniable.

"There you go, *principessa*," he murmurs, his voice low and suggestive, snapping me out of the spell he effortlessly cast.

At this point, I'm not sure if he's fucking with me or if he's suddenly making an effort, but I decide to go with it. After weeks in a home where I'm rarely spoken to, it's a welcome change. Knowing the don, it's not one I can get used to, though, but for just one evening, I allow myself to feel.

As the auction unfolds, I take on the role of Enzo's artful companion, navigating him through the curated collection up for bid. The atmosphere is charged with anticipation, reaching a crescendo when they unveil the pièce de résistance of the evening. A collective gasp ripples through the audience, echoing my own awe at the masterpiece.

"Ladies and gentlemen, in my hands rests an exquisite creation—a canvas resonating with the very essence of its creator. I urge you to embark on a journey of aesthetic revelation. The strokes, both delicate and purposeful, convey a virtuosity that transforms the ordinary into the extraordinary. The artist, a luminary among creative minds, has infused their essence into this canvas, beckoning you to unravel its secrets. This is not merely an artwork; it is a testament to the convergence of genius and passion. As the gavel hovers, ready to declare a new custodian for this opulent treasure, I encourage you to bid not just for ownership but for the privilege of becoming a steward of artistic brilliance. May the highest bidder forever intertwine themselves with the splendor of this rare and highly sought-after masterpiece. Commencing the bidding at two million dollars."

"Two million dollars for that crap?" Enzo exclaims, louder than intended, prompting curious glances from those around us. I playfully nudge him with my elbow. "Come on, that painting is far from "crap", it's incredible," I insist.

"Cecille Monroe is a rising artist, and everyone is buzzing about her work. Between her and Alexander Wong, it's impossible not to appreciate the enduring beauty of art. She's the hottest new artist on the scene and is already drawing comparisons to Willem de Kooning."

"Who?" Enzo asks, earning a chuckle from me.

"Take a moment to appreciate it... It's soft, subtle, yet harbors sharp edges. One must tread cautiously, for its beauty has the power to ensnare, leading you to lose touch with reality," I remark, unaware of how intensely Enzo is locking eyes with me.

"Much like you," he replies, his gaze still piercing into mine, sending a shiver down my spine.

Before I can utter another word, he boldly places his bid. "Five million dollars," he declares.

"Enzo, what are you doing?" I ask, utterly shocked.

"Well, you did mention it's worth more than five million, right? Thought I'd cut to the chase and secure the winning bid. Time to add a touch of sophistication to your space," he quips.

"Enzo, with five million dollars, I could buy a house," I protest.

"But darling, we already have one," he winks. As the bid

is finalized, I'm left wondering who this guy is and what he did with the jerk I left at home.

He strides over to complete the sale. "Let me secure this masterpiece for you, and I'll meet you up front, alright?" he says.

"Ummm, okay," I stammer, still in shock. After he leaves, Alexander approaches me. "I assume that's the non-boyfriend?" he asks.

I give him a light, apologetic smile as we watch the auction conclude. While Enzo invested a small fortune in one painting, Alexander also spent a considerable amount on some artwork. He sees me out of the building, following me to the car—a decision that, in hindsight, may not have been my best.

For some inexplicable reason, he's about to take my hand when the air in my lungs tightens. Even from across the parking lot, I see Enzo's face—tense lines, barely contained anger. I immediately release Alexander's hand as my heart begins to race.

"What's wrong?" he asks with concern, moving to stand in front of me. "Are you okay?"

I start to assure him, to ask him to leave, but it's too late. Enzo appears behind him, seething. His anger isn't apparent unless you know what to look for, and after three weeks of close contact, I can discern his mood.

"She's fine," Enzo snaps. Alexander turns to face him, and an uneasy tension fills the air. Both men size each other up, and worry gnaws at my gut. I understand Enzo better than anyone, aware of his capabilities.

"So, non-boyfriend, care to share your name?" Alexander questions, narrowing his brown eyes.

My jaw tightens as Enzo regards him with disdain. His eyes flare when they land on me.

"What the hell is going on here, Rosa?"

I realize I'm about to find out exactly what happens when you poke a bear. And I can't even find it in me to regret it. Because despite the means I used to get here, I now have his attention. I hadn't even realized I wanted it until now. But now that I do have it, it's up to me to decide what to do with it.

CHAPTER 9
Enzo

I 'm going to kill Jason. My day was going fine, except for Jason consistently chirping in my ear about me going to Rosa's little art show. I wasn't interested. I had better things to do. But the past few weeks, he seems to have taken it upon himself to become the champion for our smooth-sailing relationship. I told him countless times that it doesn't matter. Rosa and I both came to an arrangement, one I thought we both understood. I can see now that I was wrong.

Despite wanting to give her the space she asked for, I eventually caved and made my way here after I was done with work. When I arrived, I found the man who was supposed to be on guard asleep in the car. I fired him without hesitation, then decided to accompany her myself. Some guy was selling roses in front of the museum, so I got one for her, hoping it would get me a few extra points. But now, I'm not sure I should have come at all because I may have to kill this guy.

Control is always slipping from my grasp where she's concerned. Right now, I want nothing more than to rip her away from this man's side. Before this night, he was inconsequential. Now he's my top priority. Instead of doing something drastic like punching him in the face, I reach forward and close my arm around Rosa's wrist, pulling her to my side. The asshole moves like he wants to stop me.

"Ah, ah," I say, making a tsking sound. "I wouldn't do that if I were you. Take one more step, and you'll lose a limb."

The threat is delivered in an almost bored tone, but it has the desired effect. His feet still, and his face drains of color. Beside me, Rosa gasps softly.

"Would you tone down the dramatics?" she grits out.

"Be very careful what you say to me right now, principessa," I say without looking at her. "Leave," I order the man.

He must really have a death wish because he hesitates. My grip on Rosa's hand tightens when his brown eyes drift to her.

"It's okay," Rosa tells him, her voice soft. "I'll text you and explain everything. You can go, Alexander."

Fucking Alexander. That's the artist she was just bragging about. How fucking ironic.

"Like hell you'll text him," I growl.

She shoots me an exasperated look but thankfully "Alexander" decides to listen to her, and after one last cutting glance at me, he walks away. As soon as he does so, I lead Rosa to the car. I open the passenger door and gesture for her to enter, and she does so without complaint.

A minute later, we're driving away from the venue.

"He's a fellow artist," Rosa starts to explain after several minutes have passed. "You didn't need to threaten him like that."

"A fellow artist. The one who makes it impossible to ignore the beauty in art you said? Is that the same fellow artist you speak of?" I drawl. "Because he didn't look like that to

70

me. Not when you were staring at him with fucking hearts in your eyes. And not when he was holding onto your hand."

I stop myself before I lose control and take a few deep breathes. "You truly have a beautiful smile, Rosa. Too bad it only seems to come out around men who will probably be dead soon."

Her face blanches. "You-you can't kill him!"

"Try me," I mutter.

"No! You're being dramatic. Before tonight, I never even met him. And are you so out of touch with reality that you would rationalize murder just because I talked to another man?"

My eyes flick over to her face for a second. "Trust me, sweetheart. Eighty percent of the time, there's nothing rational about my thoughts when it comes to you. Why do you really think I chose you, Rosa?"

She looks down, "I don't know, convenience."

"You're a smart girl. You know it's more than that. Don't you?

She blows out a soft breath. "Please, don't kill him. I promise he's nothing more than a fellow artist. He and I had a conversation tonight, that's it."

I grit my teeth and stare forward, unwilling to see the vulnerability in her eyes.

"Rosa, one of these days you're going to ask me for something I can't give you," I tell her.

We ride in silence for a while until her curiosity becomes palpable. "So, why me? Out of all the women in the world, what led you to choose me? I lead a low-profile life, avoid excessive partying, and, by conventional standards, I might be considered boring and simple. So, why me?"

"Why you?" I respond with a genuine smile. "You're intelligent, stunning, and there's something about you that mesmerized me from the moment our paths crossed. I believe you felt it too, Rosa. There's no denying the undeniable chemistry between us. I sensed it immediately, and I knew right then that I needed to make you my wife. I want to follow in my father's footsteps and build my own legacy and sweetheart, there is no other woman I want by myside. It can only be you."

" I was wrong," she says gently. "I was wrong to ask you to stay away. I don't want you to."

"Do you truly mean that, principessa? Or are you just saying it so I'll spare your friend?"

She responds with a playful tone, "Well, you did just splurge five million dollars on artwork for me, so it's only fair I let you swing by my room and take a peek at it from time to time."

Then, more seriously, she continues, "I mean it. I shouldn't have lashed out at you the way I did the other day, and I'm sorry." My anger has subsided. She goes on, "I've had some time to think, and you were right. We should, at the very least, try to make this marriage work. We owe it to ourselves to give it a chance."

"As long as I don't kill your friend," I mutter in distaste.

"If you kill him, I'll never forgive you," Rosa says firmly.

I let out a sigh. "Alright, fine. You drive a hard bargain, Miss De Luca. But I'll adhere to your terms."

She immediately relaxes. When I look at her, she's actually smiling. A real, genuine smile. I guess it helps to know that she's more than a bargaining chip. I knew she would be mine the moment her photo slid across my desk. My heart actually stutters at the sight. Not that it's all her fault but if she did that a lot more often, I'd be more inclined to want to spend more time in her presence. To want to drag out more from her.

Instead of driving us home, I take a detour, driving toward a restaurant I have a feeling she might like. When we arrive, Rosa arches an eyebrow.

"What's going on?"

"A date," I reply, taking off my seatbelt. "I'm taking you up on your offer to try to make this marriage work."

Her expression turns pensive. "Twice in one day? What if someone sees us? I thought we were keeping this under wraps until you're ready to make an official announcement."

"I don't particularly care about that anymore, Rosa."

Wanting to keep us a secret is the only reason a fucker like Alexander could even think to come close to what's mine.

"Plus, if this is going to be believable we might as well be seen in public together a few times."

She nods in understanding. I exit the car, moving to open her door. When she steps out, she even allows me to hold her hand. It's progress. I try but fail to ignore how right her hand feels in mine. It's dainty, small, but also perfect. Like I was always meant to hold her.

Inside the restaurant, we're offered seats in a private area. We start talking after ordering some wine and food, and I realize Rosa has some burning questions. Some she can't wait to get out.

"If I ask you something, promise you won't bite my head off?"

"That remains to be seen, sweetheart. I do have a tendency to grow fangs every full moon," I say drolly.

She laughs. "You know what I meant."

"Fire away."

"Where did you stay? Before you took over as Don. You weren't in the U.S."

My gut instinct is to divert the question, hide my truths,

keep them under lock and key. But she's not asking because she wants to use what I say against me. She's genuinely curious, and she's right. If we want this to work, we have to try to get to know each other. It can't be one-sided.

"I was in London for a while when I was nineteen. Then I went to Italy, South Africa. I visited a lot of countries, actually. Never really settled in one place."

"Why not? Were you running from something?" she asks softly.

I shake my head. Nothing. Everything.

The demons of my past. The expectations of my future. I was running from my responsibility, trying to ignore my duty. For a little while, I succeeded, until I couldn't take it anymore and I knew I had to come back.

Rosa doesn't press the question. I think she can see in my eyes that I can't provide an answer because she moves on swiftly to her next one.

"So, if you're so well-traveled, how many languages can you speak?"

I pause to think on it for a second. "Six," I reply.

Her eyes widen. "No way. How do you know six languages? Which ones?"

I list them for her. "Italian, English, Spanish, French. Those are the ones I can speak fluently. Then I know some Portuguese from staying in Brazil for a while. And I picked up on some Chinese as well, but I'm not as fluent."

"That's... impressive," she says with a small smile.

"My IQ is remarkably high. I pick up a lot of things easily," I state.

"Humble brag," she mutters with a smirk. "Maybe you could teach me some French sometime. I've always loved to hear it."

"Sure, sweetheart." I smirk. "I'll whisper it in your ear every night before you fall asleep."

Her cheeks redden when the implication of my words lands. She clears her throat and looks away from me. I lean back in my chair with a smile. Conversation thankfully shifts to her and her life. She tells me a little about growing up. Her brother, her family. Then I decide to ask her something I've always been curious about.

"When did you start learning pottery? It's not a hobby many people cultivate. And you not only cultivated it but you thrived. How did you start out?"

Rosa pauses for a second. I see a slight flicker of hesitation in her blue eyes before she crushes it.

"I was pretty isolated as a child. While my father was grooming Roman to take over the family business, I was mostly left alone. No one really paid any attention to me. I know they all loved me, but my dad treated me like just another one of his possessions, and my brother treated me like something he had to protect. And my mother, she was the probably the worst. She treated me like a project. She raised me to be perfect. The perfect daughter, the perfect sister, and finally, the perfect wife."

There's a hint of bitterness in her tone.

"I know she did it to protect me. In her eyes, that was the best way to prepare me for the world we live in. I had to do everything right. And when there's a strong weight of expectation on you, it starts to feel crushing. I needed an escape. Some form of freedom. And I've always liked art. Even as a little kid, I loved to draw, to create things. My mother took me to an event one day where there were so many different artists showcasing their talents. I was drawn to the potter. Something about what he did called to me, the way he molded the clay with his hands.

The process was intriguing. I asked my mother for the tools to practice before I went to bed that day. When I got home from school a few days later, I had everything I needed and I blossomed from there. Pottery's an outlet for me," she says softly.

"You haven't worked on it since you moved in," I point out. "Did you need me to set something up for you?"

She shakes her head. "No, it's okay. I'm still trying to figure all of this out and would rather deal with it head-on. Like I said, art is a means of escape for me. A way to express my feelings without going crazy. I guess you could say it's my therapy but, I think I should face this head-on so I know what I'm really getting into."

"So you're saying you're okay right now?" I ask her..

"I love being a potter, but it doesn't define my entire being. I exist apart from it. I don't know if you... if you understand that?" she asks.

"Yeah, I get it, *principessa*."

More than she'll ever know. Better than anyone, I understand having a means of escape and not letting it rule you or control you. Not letting yourself become dependent on it.

We spend the rest of the evening eating our meal and engaging in small talk. I can't remember the last time I did something so domesticated. But it's worth it, though. I tell myself it just has to be worth it. Otherwise, everything I've ever wanted, everything I've built will crumble.

There also can't be any other reasons.

———

OUR ENGAGEMENT TAKES place a week later. Rosa's in her bedroom when I knock on her door. It's pretty late, but I was hoping to do this today and be done with it. When she opens it, my breath catches. Moonlight plays across her skin, a reflection from the open window in her room. It makes her glow. Her waves of hair spread out across her face. She's only in a thin tank top, which barely conceals the rise and fall of her breasts.

"Enzo?" she asks. "What are you doing here?"

Apart from that first day, she has never been in my bedroom and vice versa. Despite both rooms being extremely close to each other.

"I need to talk to you. Can I come in?"

"Sure," she says, moving from the doorway.

I step inside the large room and the door clicks shut behind me. My gaze drifts across the room but I barely take in anything as I turn around to look at her. I can't not look at her. I clench my jaw, trying to distract myself from her nipples, which are hard and visible beneath her tank top. Her eyes widen when she notices. She blushes, grabbing a robe from the corner of her bed. I don't stop her as she pulls it on.

Much better. At least now I can focus on what I came here to do.

"Remember when you said you wanted to make this marriage work?" I ask her.

She nods once, expression growing worried.

"Well, I'm going to take that as a sign that you don't have as many doubts as you did when you first moved in. I was trying to give you some time to get used to life here, but I think we've used up enough time."

"What are you talking about?" she asks, voice soft.

"Here." I offer her a small velvet box.

She accepts it from my hands, and I watch as she opens it. "Holy shit."

A chuckle escapes me. "I thought we might get engaged officially."

She looks at me, something vulnerable in the depths of her eyes.

"Enzo, this ring is… it's beautiful," she breathes. "I wasn't expecting something like this."

"It belonged to my mother," I inform her. "I had it taken out of our family vault today. She was the last person to wear it. Before she… she died. And now I want you to wear it. Despite our beginning and the reason for this match, you're going to be my wife and I want to build a strong foundation for our legacy. Besides, she would have wanted you to wear it."

Rosa nods, her expression still dumbfounded. When her eyes meet mine, I can tell she's touched.

"Damn, Enzo. I didn't know you had a romantic in you," she murmurs.

"I'm not getting down on one knee, of course."

"Of course," she echoes with a small smile. "But you could put it on."

She hands me the box and stretches her hand at me. I swallow before taking a hold of her hand. Very gently, I remove the ring and slide it onto her finger. It's a small diamond with tiny sapphires lining the edges. I imagine it cost a fortune, and that's without taking into account the sentimental value involved.

I almost didn't give it to her. Convinced myself to buy her another ring instead. But she's worth it. I need her to be worth it.

When her gaze lifts to mine, a ripple of lust slithers through me. And then Rosa makes it worse.

"Traditionally, all that's left is a kiss," she says softly. "To seal the deal."

"To seal the deal," I repeat, amused.

Panic flares in her blue eyes. "You don't have to, of

course. I just-I wanted us to at least…" She stops her rambling and rubs a hand over her eyes. "Just forget it. You can go," she mutters.

"Rosa." Her name comes out rough, tinged with desire. "Shut up."

I pull her closer and count three heartbeats. We both pause. Waiting. I'm trying to convince myself it's a mistake, to convince myself not to. My hand traces the diamond on her finger. Her breaths come out in soft pants.

I really shouldn't do this.

But at the end of the day, when her hazy gaze meets mine and I see my own lust mirrored there, I know I have no other choice.

Fuck control. My hand goes up to her face and my head lowers as I capture her lips in mine.

CHAPTER 10
Rosa

For what feels like a lifetime but is actually only a few seconds, I can hardly breathe. Because Enzo is kissing me. My eyes are wide and panic courses through my veins. Panic and something else. He's so close his eyes glimmer. I've always known he's good-looking, but now the sight of him hits me like a blow to my chest, spreading warmth through me.

"Rosa," he says against my lips. "Kiss me back."

The words are a plea. And they effectively bring me back to the present. The commanding pressure of his hand on my face feels like fire in my blood, slicing lower to the wetness pooling between my legs. My lips part, and that's all the opening he needs.

Enzo kisses me like a man starved. I've been kissed before, but not like this. He kisses me like I'm the oxygen he needs to survive, each slide of his lips searing against my heart. I grab onto his shoulders, afraid of letting go. Because if I do, if I let go, I'll fall. And I'm not sure I could get back up.

I grab a fistful of his hair, holding him even closer as I

drag his mouth to mine and slide my tongue between his lips. Enzo lets out a soft hiss before lifting me so I can wrap my legs around his hips. He moves until he's pressing me against the wall. Need pours through me in thick waves. I moan softly against his lips.

I can feel his hard erection between my thighs. I can't stop myself from grinding against him, desperate for the friction.

"Fuck," Enzo groans, wrenching his mouth from mine.

I blink, staring up at him. My heart is still running a marathon and I'm not sure how to stop it. We're both breathless. Enzo's jaw tightens as he looks at me. He lets out a soft breath and leans down, pressing his forehead against mine.

"It was a good idea to put on that robe, *principessa*," he whispers. "A really good idea."

I slide down from his body, keeping my back against the wall because my legs currently feel like jelly. It's actually ridiculous that a mere kiss made me feel that way. He barely even touched me.

My cheeks are hot and my body feels like there's a fire racing through it. Enzo's expression is slightly pained as he watches me. He runs a hand through his hair, making the reddish-brown strands stick up.

"I think that as far as traditional kisses go, we did our best," he finally says.

"A-plus," I reply softly with a nod, unable to stop staring at him.

A muscle ticks in his jaw and finally he looks away. "Good night, Rosa."

Before I can blink, he's walking out the door. I finally allow myself to slide down to the ground. I place my head in my hands and groan softly.

What the heck have I just done?

I DON'T GO DOWN for breakfast the next day. I stay put in my bed until I'm sure Enzo has left the house. I'm too mortified to face him. By noon, my stomach is growling and I decide I'm not mortified enough to die of hunger. Plus, he should be gone by now. I get dressed and head downstairs to the kitchen. As soon as I make a turn in the hallway, I find myself in the path of two women.

Isabella's blue eyes narrow onto me, but she's not the one that has me freezing in place. Denise Russo has dark brown hair and brown eyes. She can't be more than forty. But right now, she looks much older, with lines drawn across her face and wrinkles around her mouth and eyes. She looks sick. But when her eyes meet mine, there's no mistaking the anger there.

I haven't seen her since moving here. When I asked Jason, he said she didn't like to leave her room. I didn't realize it was because she was ill. Isabella holds onto her arm. She's even unsteady on her feet.

Oh, god. What's wrong with her?

"Nice bling, Rosario," Isabella says, eyes fixed on the diamond on my fingers.

My instinct is to hide my hand behind my back. Which is wrong. I've done nothing wrong.

Denise's brown eyes move to the diamond as well, and I watch as she studies it for several seconds. When she looks back up at me, there's even more anger in her gaze.

She has every right to be angry. Roman killed her husband. But this is the Cosa Nostra. She has to know that I had no control over that. Just like she didn't. She's currently the oldest member of this family, and the least I can do is accord her some respect.

"Mrs. Russo," I say gently. "It's really nice to finally meet you."

She laughs. It's brittle and cold. "Do you even understand the significance of the ring on your finger?" she asks. Her voice is surprisingly strong. "That ring has been in this family for generations. It belongs to the first-born son of the Russos. The next in line to become Don."

I arch an eyebrow. "Isn't Enzo a first-born son?"

Unless there's another son out there that I have no idea about. Knowing this family, it's entirely possible.

"No," Denise replies bitterly. "I merely wanted to point out that neither you nor Enzo deserves to be in that position. That ring should have belonged to me or Isabella's mother. It's insulting that it's on the finger of someone like you."

Well, that's harsh.

"You don't even know me, Denise," I say calmly.

"I don't need to," she states. Then she looks at Isabella beside her. "Let's go, Isa. I'm tired of the present company."

Isabella shoots me an annoyed look like I'm somehow at fault. Wrapping her arms around Denise's shoulders, she escorts the woman away.

As far as first interactions go, every single one with nearly every member of this family has been next to awful. It hits me that the only meeting that was actually nice was with Enzo. And that was only because I didn't know who he was at first.

I spend the rest of the day replying to emails and watching TV. By the time evening rolls around, I'm actively anticipating Enzo's return. This morning, I would have done anything to avoid him thanks to our kiss last night, but I have questions now. Questions that require answers.

As soon as I hear his footsteps, I climb off my bed and

head for the door. When I open it, Enzo's leaning against the wall on the other side, a contemplative expression on his face.

"Hey," I say. "What are you doing there?"

"We need to talk," he informs me.

I nod, despite the nerves blossoming in the pit of my stomach.

"Yeah. I need to talk to you, as well. I wanted to ask about Denise."

A dark brown eyebrow flicks up. "Denise?"

"Yes. Your aunt. Did you know she's sick?"

"You saw her?"

"Earlier today," I confirm. "I think she was going on a walk with Isabella. Enzo, she... she doesn't look well."

He sighs. "I know. Losing her husband was a pretty big blow. I tried to help her, but she doesn't trust me. She has a doctor come in to check up on her. I talked to him once and he told me she would get better eventually. I can't interfere further than that. What did she say to you?"

I shake my head. "Nothing."

"Liar. She probably talked about how much I didn't deserve my position. Which is ridiculous because it's my fucking birthright." Enzo chuckles. "Her husband and his brother were never meant to be in charge. They didn't have what it took and they paid for it."

"Still, you can't blame her for feeling the way she does," I murmur. "You did have her husband killed."

"He was dead anyway," Enzo states. "All I did was speed up the process. If you ask me, I got him a merciful death. Knowing your brother, he would have been tortured for a long time before he was finally killed."

I clench my jaw, trying hard not to think about his words.

"It makes you uncomfortable, doesn't it?" Enzo questions. There's a small smirk on his face as he pushes off the wall and moves to stand in front of me. He's still in his suit, although he has ditched the jacket. The sleeves of his shirt are rolled up. I swallow softly when his arm reaches up and he gently runs his hand through my hair.

"We kill people, *principessa*, he says softly. "You were born into the Cosa Nostra. You should be used to it by now."

I look him straight in the eye, "I'm not a murderer. And I'll never be okay with what you do. The only thing I can do is ignore it."

He smiles. "You'll be ignoring it for the rest of your life, then. It's a pity; I kind of wanted a wife who was a bit more… supportive."

I glare at him and shift out of his grip. His hand closes up in a fist and he steps back toward the wall.

"What did you want to talk about?" I ask him.

"Our kiss," he replies bluntly.

His expression doesn't so much as flicker. Meanwhile, my heart skips several beats.

"What about it?" I ask in the most normal voice I can muster.

"I realized we didn't set some ground rules."

"Ground rules," I repeat dryly.

"Yeah. In case you didn't notice, sweetheart, I thrive on control. I really fucking hate it when things throw me off. And our kiss last night…" he trails off. "I just want us to have a clear idea of where we stand."

I hate the way he's treating this. Clinical. Like a business arrangement. Which, at the end of the day, this whole thing actually is. A sham that I have to tie myself to forever. It slipped my mind for a minute. Anger flares in my chest.

I raise my chin as I stare at him. "You don't have to worry about your precious control. And if it's ground rules you want, here's one: We won't kiss again unless it's in public in order to prove the legitimacy of our marriage. Apart from that, you can leave me the fuck alone."

Heat flares in his eyes. "There's no need to get mad, sweetheart."

"Stop calling me that," I snap.

He runs a hand through his hair. "I didn't come here for a fight."

"I know. You came to establish your precious control. Don't worry, I understand you perfectly. Anything else you'd like to talk about?"

I can tell he wants to say something else, but he seems to convince himself not to.

"You received an invitation to La Mirage in a few days, right?" he asks.

"Yes. Why?"

La Mirage is an exclusive event held annually for New York's socialites. As a member of one of the big mafia families, I receive an invitation every year. I don't usually go, though. Mostly because there's always a fight being broken up at the event before the end of the night.

Men's egos can be annoyingly delicate. And putting most of the rich, powerful, and influential people of New York in one room is bound to end up in some form of disaster or the other.

"We're going together," Enzo informs me. "Our chance to announce our engagement."

I'm not in the mood for an argument, so all I do is offer him a short nod. "Fine. Is that all?"

"Yeah."

"Good night, Enzo." I turn to go back to my room, then pause, realizing something. Very carefully, I turn around. "Quick question, though, do you plan to remain celibate for the rest of your life?"

His lips curl into a smile. "And why the fuck would I be celibate?"

"We just agreed on intimacy only when necessary and in public. I'm just concerned that all that solo action might lead to some issues."

"Don't worry, principessa," he says with a smirk. "I'm sure we can figure out a way to make that arrangement work."

I'm taken aback by his response. "Meaning?"

He approaches me, and my breath catches as he gently shifts some hair from my forehead.

"Good night, Rosa."

He walks away, leaving me with more questions than answers. I curl my lips in distaste. Of all people, my brother had to arrange my marriage to the most annoyingly vague and obscure man ever.

CHAPTER 11

Enzo

I haven't had a lot of experience dealing with people. I grew up isolated. Isabella was the only real company I had until I turned eighteen, and since then, I haven't really had anyone. I guess I've had Jason, but our relationship never actually progressed into the realm of talking through our feelings. Especially now that I'm his boss.

I can assemble a Rubix's Cube in less than twenty minutes. I'm an expert at about three or four forms of martial arts. I'd say I pick shit up pretty easily and dominate everything that I do. But when it comes to human feelings, I'm woefully inept. Which is why the state in which Rosa and I have found ourselves in presently is extremely annoying.

One step forward, two steps back. And I have no fucking clue how to bridge that gap.

"Uncle Enzo," Maria says, barging into my thoughts.

"Hm?" I reply, my eyes meeting hers through the rearview mirror.

I'm driving them to school since their normal driver is unavailable. Isabella is seated beside me, because she doesn't trust me to deliver our little cousins safely. I'm honestly over her attitude. And it hits me that if I can't manage to repair my relationship with my family, it's highly likely I won't be able to with Rosa either.

"Is Rosa your girlfriend?" Maria questions with a small smile.

Surprisingly, her brother speaks up as well. "When she came, you said she would be your wife. But our teacher says you can't have a wife unless you've had a wedding. So are you and Rosa married?"

"We're not married yet, guys. But we will be. We're engaged, so right now she's my fiancée."

They fall silent, their expressions contemplative.

"So when will you get married?" Maria asks.

I pause to think about it. That's a conversation we haven't had. We probably should, as soon as we navigate through the stormy water we're currently in.

"Before the end of the year," I inform the twins. "Probably in the winter."

Isabella's gaze cuts to mine. "Who has a winter wedding?"

"Why? Worried it'll be too cold for you?"

"That would mean I had plans to come to your stupid wedding and I don't," she mutters with a frown.

"I want to go to the wedding," Maria says. "Can I wear a pretty dress to the wedding? Please, Isa?"

Isabella lets out a soft sigh. "Of course, my darling. You'll go to Enzo's wedding."

"You'll go, too?" Matthew asks hopefully.

She rolls her eyes. "Sure."

The twins are perfectly happy as we drop them off at school. Isabella watches them enter the building with a sad smile on her face.

"I'm glad they're happy again. They were so sad after

their papa passed. I was worried they wouldn't recover."

My jaw clenches. "Of course. Kids are resilient. Until they're not."

She looks at me and something cracks in her expression. "Enzo…"

"Whatever you're going to say, don't," I tell her.

Of all the people in my life, Isabella understands what I went through best. But that doesn't mean I want to reminisce about old times.

"You and Rosa," she says instead. "You might want to fix whatever it is you've done."

I arch an eyebrow. "And why do you care?"

"I don't. But despite what you may think, I don't *hate* you cousin. I know we've all been dealing with some pretty fucked up things in this family and since you're the don, you get to carry the burden. However… I have seen some light in you these past few weeks and I suppose you have Rosa to thank for that. I'm just saying… I don't want you to let the only good thing in your life go to shits. I'm pretty sure the woman you're supposed to be getting married to is meant to be able to look you in the eye."

My gaze falls forward as I take in her words. "We'll figure it out," I say.

Unfortunately, I just might have been talking out of my own ass. Because my fiancée insists on being the most infuriating person on the planet.

"I'm not going with you," Rosa repeats, chin raised, that stubborn flare in her eyes.

I stare at her incredulously. "You do realize this is supposed to be our debut into New York society."

She makes a face. "Stop talking like that. You make it sound like we're some old regency couple."

I consider that. "Okay, you may have a point," I agree. "Now, tell me why you're suddenly not going to La Mirage."

"I'm going. I'm just not going with you."

I take a deep, calming breath. We're standing at the entrance to her bedroom. I just told her a few minutes ago to get ready for the party she agreed to attend days ago.

"Rosa. We're engaged. Why the fuck would we not go together?"

She hesitates. Something flickers in the blue depths of her eyes. "I just… I just can't be in a car with you right now," she finally says.

"Why not? I'm not going to maul you, sweetheart. Surely you can manage a car ride for less than an hour."

She rolls her eyes. "Oh yeah, how long till we start arguing? Or something worse. I don't have the energy for that tonight."

I pause, studying her expression. Her cheeks are flushed. She looks away at my perusal. And suddenly, I understand what's wrong.

"You're a terrible liar, principessa. That's not what you're really worried about, is it?"

When I take a step forward, her breath catches. My voice goes low. "What do you think I'm going to do? Kiss you? Do you want me to?"

I could move closer to her. Make good on that request. The number of things I could do to her. The things I want to do to her. But I've been refraining. Because, like it or not, this is a delicate situation. And the least I can do is not rush things.

Rosa's mine. She's not going anywhere.

Her hands curl into fists. "You're being ridiculous. We had a deal."

"I'm pretty sure I told you I didn't agree to that," I state. "Tell me, sweetheart, what are you so afraid of?"

"You know my brother asked me that. Before I moved here. He asked me what I was scared of," she says softly.

"What did you say?"

"I told him I was scared of everything."

"Even me?"

"Especially you. That hasn't changed, Enzo. I've lived in your house for nearly two months. And that hasn't changed," she says sadly.

I blow out a breath. "Well, that's unfortunate."

She lets out a soft laugh. "You think?"

FOR ALL HER HESITATION, Rosa's practically perfect beside me. As soon as we arrive at the party, we're approached by several people wondering why we're together. She's great at playing her part. She makes sure to dangle her diamond in front of their eager gazes, laughs at their stupid jokes, and accepts every compliment graciously. She's not thrown off when people raise eyebrows at our sudden engagement.

I want to tell them to fuck off.

"You're scaring people," Rosa whispers to me. "Quit brooding."

"I don't brood," I mutter. "I'm just not a fan of crowds."

"Or people," she adds.

"Hey, I like you plenty," I say, rubbing our shoulders together.

"Could have fooled me," she says.

But at least she smiles. Which is progress. After several

more long minutes of annoying questions and petty conversation, we're able to retreat to a corner. I grab a glass of champagne from a passing waiter's tray and hand it to her.

Rosa offers me a grateful smile. For a second, one painfully long heartbeat, I just stare at her. Her long glossy black hair that has been curled at the tips. Her glowing olive skin, her gorgeous face. And the dress she's wearing. I simultaneously want to burn it and keep it on her forever. It's dark red and clings to every single sexy curve on her body. It flows down to the ground, but there's a long slit in front reaching up to her mid-thigh.

It's driving me crazy. When she's done with her champagne, her eyes lift to mine.

"I think we should probably dance," I tell her.

"Oh, joy," she says sarcastically.

I chuckle. "You don't want to?"

"I will. As long as you promise not to kiss me," she says warily.

She's really thinking about this. I would be worried if I wasn't so glad that our kiss seems to be plaguing her as much as it's plaguing me.

"Don't worry, sweetheart," I lean down to whisper the next words in her ear, "I won't kiss you. Unless…you ask me to."

I pretend not to notice the way she shivers. When I hold out my hand, she grudgingly accepts. I lead her to the dance floor and for the next few minutes, everything else falls away but us. I'm keenly aware of the feel of her in my arms. She keeps her face against my shoulder, her eyes not meeting mine.

"My dad taught me how to slow dance when I was little," she says. "It's times like this I miss him the most."

"He was a wonderful man," I tell her.

"You didn't even know him."

"Like I keep telling you, *principessa*, I know everything."

She lets out a soft gasp followed by a laugh when I push her gently backward and twirl her before pulling her back. When she's in my arms again, her eyes finally meet mine.

It makes sense that I'd be attracted to her. She's an incredibly beautiful woman. And we're going to get married. Sexual attraction makes sense. But what doesn't make sense is the way my heart speeds up when her eyes meet mine like this. Or the part of me that wants to know everything about her. What drives her. Her secret thoughts. Her dreams. And, most importantly, how to win her heart.

Every moment I spend with Rosa is a moment closer to me being fucked.

After our dance, we walk back to her family and friends. The D'Angelos have joined our little group. Rosa excitedly hugs Daniella D'Angelo, who seems a little angry. I don't listen in on their conversation; I'm too busy watching Christian D'Angelo.

He's talking to Roman. I've never met him, but the man's a legend in the Cosa Nostra. A powerful Don. Someone I could respect. He and Roman were true to their legacies. They made sure to protect the empires their fathers left them —something I couldn't do. It wasn't in my control at the time.

Both men look up at me, stalling their conversation.

"Christian," Roman starts, "this is Enzo Russo. My future brother-in-law."

"I heard," Christian says dryly.

He appears to be sizing me up. I arch an eyebrow at him.

"I've heard a lot about you, too. Exactly how were you able to find out about the vineyard sale before everyone else?"

"Vineyard" in this case is code for heroin field. We're in public, after all.

Christian smirks. "I guess it just goes to show how much better than you I am."

That draws a chuckle from me. I knew I'd like him.

"Maybe," I agree. "For now. Tread carefully, D'Angelo. There's a new Don in town."

"I can drink to that," he says with a short nod. "I look forward to seeing what you do. Good luck."

"Thanks."

Roman speaks up. "Now that you're done bonding, do you guys want to hit the bar? I swear these events get more boring every time I come."

"They're not so bad," I say, my eyes trailing over the numerous men and women wearing all sorts of luxury items and precious gems.

It was a good idea not to bring Jason along. He gets irritated when he sees opulence and extravagance so casually displayed. He barely had anything to eat as a child.

"I've been going to these events for years, trust me, man. They're terrible."

We decide to head to the bar, but before that, I catch Rosa's eye. She breaks apart from Elena and Daniella and moves over.

"You good?" I ask and she nods.

"Yeah."

She actually does look happy. There's color in her cheeks and a brightness in her eyes. It's pretty clear she loves being surrounded by her family and friends.

"I'm going to the bar with the guys," I inform her. "Do you want to come with me?" I ask as an afterthought.

"No. Dany and I are going to the restroom. I'll come find you later."

For some inexplicable reason, worry spreads through me. "Be careful. There's a lot of people here."

And not all of them are friendly. I'm really starting to regret not bringing extra security.

"I'll be fine," she says, shooting me a look like I'm being unreasonable.

She goes back to her friends and I head to the bar. We're joined by Christian's brother, Topher, and they start talking about some exclusive club that I should join but I'm only half listening. After one shot of vodka, I'm turning around, my eyes seeking out Rosa. Both she and Daniella are still missing. I make it another few minutes before I slip away, heading out of the ballroom.

I'm about to turn to the hallway leading to the restroom when I hear their voices.

"You've been avoiding the question all night, Rosa. But seriously, why am I sensing so much tension between you and your fiancé who you supposedly dislike?" Daniella questions.

Seeing as I'm the topic of discussion, I decide to lean against the wall and wait for them to appear.

"Because we want to kill each other," Rosa says blandly.

"Yeah, right," Daniella scoffs. "More like rip each other's clothes off. The sexual tension the two of you were radiating could melt a person's face off. Please, tell me you've slept together."

"We haven't."

"But you want to," Daniella says suggestively.

I unfortunately don't get to hear Rosa's reply because both women happen to appear at that moment. Rosa's eyes widen as she takes me in. She gets over her shock pretty quickly, though.

"Enzo, you do realize it's rude to eavesdrop," she says, her cheeks red.

My shoulders lift in a shrug. "I wasn't eavesdropping. I just happened to overhear your conversation."

"Which is eavesdropping. What are you doing out here? I'm perfectly capable of going to the ladies' room on my own," she bites out.

"Never said you weren't, sweetheart. But you were gone a long time."

"Because we were talking. You have huge control issues," she mutters.

"Hi," Daniella D'Angelo speaks up from beside her. I turn to the redhead with a raised eyebrow. "I'm Daniella. We haven't met."

"Yeah," I say coolly. "Nice to meet you."

Her expression is thoughtful for a moment before she smiles. "You're even more intense than Christian. Which I didn't think was possible."

I cock my head to the side. "Did you just compare me to your husband?"

"Maybe," she drawls. "Anyway, it was nice to meet you, too. I'll head back inside, Rosa."

Rosa's glaring at me and I know she's going for intimidating but all I can think about in that moment is how fucking sexy she looks. And how I really do want to rip her clothes off.

"I'm sorry for mistakenly overhearing your conversation," I say in the most apologetic tone I can muster.

She rolls her eyes. "You're annoying."

"Careful, Rosa." I smile. "If I didn't know better, I'd think you were warming up to me."

"As if. Come on, let's go back in. Since it's clear you will continue to worry obsessively, I'll stay by your side for the rest of the night."

Something warm slides through my chest. "Yeah, you definitely like me now."

"Don't push your luck."

CHAPTER 12
Rosa

My brother wraps his arm around my waist, pulling me into a hug. I inhale, feeling soft and cushioned because no matter what, I'll always be safe in his arms. He pulls away and offers me a small smile.

"You're coming over for wedding prep in a few days right?" he asks and I nod.

"I already promised Lena."

They're getting married in two weeks and it's so surreal and exciting. I'm really happy for my brother. If someone had asked me a year ago what I thought about my brother becoming a father, the word I would have used is "worried."

Roman is the best: caring, protective, loving, responsible. But he has been carrying a huge weight on his shoulders practically since the moment he was born. Especially after my dad died. My worries had more to do with the fact that I didn't want that weight to double, especially if he added someone else to the people he felt he needed to be responsible for. I didn't want him to crash and burn.

But he didn't crash and burn—he soared. And my heart

warms every day knowing that he found his person. That he found love.

He definitely deserves it.

"Mom misses you. I can't believe you haven't seen her since you moved out," Roman says, his voice lightly scolding.

I look away and shrug. I've spoken to my mom a few times over the phone, but she hasn't apologized. I'm not sure she even understands that what she did was wrong.

Roman gives me a meaningful look. "Holding grudges, *sorella*."

"I just have a lot going on," I inform him.

"Yeah, about that. How's it going with Russo? Is he treating you right?"

Enzo's walking over now. We were leaving when he was pulled into a conversation with a couple of people from the party. I followed Roman and Elena outside to say goodbye. Elena's already in the car waiting for him.

"Everything's fine," I assure my brother.

I don't have the heart to tell him that's a lie. Because two months later, it feels like Enzo and I have barely made any progress.

Roman looks at me like he doesn't quite believe me but he doesn't push. "Make sure to work out your issues with Mom when you come over," he says just as Enzo appears beside him.

"I will. Bye, big brother."

He winks at me before looking at Enzo beside him. They offer each other weird bro nods and then Roman walks away, joining his fiancée at the car.

"What was that about your mother?" Enzo asks immediately.

He moves to my side. We start walking toward our car and he wraps his arm around my waist. I'm acutely aware of his touch. And even worse, I like the feel of his hands on me. I can't help but think about how many times my body reacted to him tonight. Every look, every touch—it was like he was trying to imprint himself into me. I felt everything.

Enzo has always been intense. But tonight, any time our eyes met, it felt like he was finally letting me see the real him. The person he keeps hidden from the rest of the world.

But he has never let me see that person. And it would be wishful thinking to imagine he would.

"Nothing. We've just been in a kind of fight," I say to answer his question.

"About?"

When we reach the black BMW, Enzo opens the passenger door for me. I find myself analyzing it. He has impeccable manners. A perfect gentleman. Or at least that's how he seems. But that's the problem. Everything Enzo does is deliberate, a way to paint himself as someone other than who he truly he is. I don't know if I know him. And that's our greatest issue.

I enter the car and wait for him to settle in the driver's seat before replying.

"I was just disappointed by her reaction when she heard about our match," I state with a small shrug.

Roman's expression grows thoughtful. "What reaction?"

"It doesn't matter. Anyway, I'm not angry at her anymore. I'm actually excited to see her in a few days. She must be stressed from all the wedding preparations."

Enzo looks like he has something more to say but he doesn't. Instead, he turns, facing forward to start the car. We arrive home in less than thirty minutes. It hits me then that

I've acclimated enough to the Russo home to start referring to it as mine. The walls are silent, the house dimly lit as we walk across the floors.

Enzo follows me as we head in the direction of our bedrooms. Once I reach mine, I think he's going to continue walking along, but he stays put. Nerves billow through me and I turn around.

"What is it?"

"We need to talk, Rosa," he says softly, his blue eyes intent, serious.

I shiver at the weight of his gaze on me.

"Do we really?" I ask nervously, because there's only one thing he could possibly want to talk about right now. "It's late and I'm tired."

Enzo's lips curl in amusement. "I'm sure you'll survive a few minutes of conversation."

"Will it really be a few minutes, though?" I toss back, my tone daring.

He shrugs. "That depends on you, sweetheart."

I sigh, opening my door. "Fine, let's talk."

He follows me into the room, shutting the door behind him. I immediately head for my bed, kicking off my heels as I do so. Enzo leans against the wall, putting some distance between us. He ditched his black suit jacket and tie before we started driving home, and he looks annoyingly good with his shirt sleeves rolled up and the first two buttons of his shirt undone.

"Well?" I ask when the silence starts to grow uncomfortable. "You had something to say?"

Enzo nods slowly, his eyes fixed on mine. "I'm just trying to work something out in my head."

"Which is?" I question.

"Okay, so, when we first met officially, after you found

out about the contract, you said something. You said you wanted better for yourself. At the time, I didn't really care about what you said. But I do now." His eyes are filled with heat as he asks. "What did you mean by that?"

I'm caught off guard by the question. I wasn't expecting it, and I'm not even sure why he's asking when I know for a fact that he knows the answer.

Regardless, I take a deep breath before replying. "I guess I always wanted something different. My parents were in an arranged marriage. And while they eventually grew to love each other, that love was punctuated more by duty. Men in our family, men in the outfit, they tend to view their women as their own personal possessions, theirs to protect—"

"As they should," Enzo murmurs.

I glare at him to keep quiet. "Anyway, that's how my parents' relationship felt sometimes. Like duty, responsibility. And I didn't want that. A part of me has always known I might not have a choice in my marriage, but I dared to hope. I've always wanted a love that was pure, not motivated by duty or responsibility. I wanted someone that cared for me because of me. Not because he was honor-bound to do so. Not because he bought me in a contract," I say softly.

Enzo flinches. It's almost imperceptible, but I notice. A muscle ticks in his jaw as he looks away from me.

"I guess we've been doomed from the start," he mutters.

"No. That's not what I'm trying to say," I say, getting to my feet. My heart pounds with each step I take toward him. "I did want better for myself, and I still do. We're not there yet, but despite the start to my parents' relationship, they still loved each other. It might have been muted, but it was still love. And I want love, too. Maybe not like theirs, but a love that I can call my own."

Pain flashes in Enzo's expression. "Rosa, I don't know how to give you what you want."

My chest rises and falls with each passing second. "You can try. No, scratch that, you're going to fucking try. Because I might not have had much of a choice in choosing you, but I choose you now and you're going to work hard to be better. Got it?"

He smiles. "I have to say, not a lot of people give me orders with the words 'got it' attached at the end."

"Get used to it," I say with a smile of my own. I even stick my tongue out at him playfully.

Enzo's eyes darken. "Don't stick your tongue out at me, *principessa*. It makes me want to suck it into my mouth."

My breath hitches. As soon as he says it, the temperature in the room goes up a couple degrees. I can tell he realizes it was the wrong thing to say. Or maybe the right thing because I'm made increasingly aware of the lust simmering within me. My carefully controlled feelings for him.

"What's stopping you?" I ask breathlessly.

Our eyes lock, spreading sparks across my skin. My chest grows heavy as my heart starts to race. We both move at the same time. His lips meet mine and almost immediately, my pulse thrums between my legs. His teeth drag across my bottom lip in a way that drives me wild. One of his hands wraps around the back of my neck, trapping me against him as he kisses me. My body shudders from his touch.

I shut my eyes, relishing the sensation of his lips against mine. His hand trails down to my ass and I gasp when he squeezes.

"Fuck, so soft," he says against my lips.

The desire inside me grows to new heights. He continues to explore my lips like a man on a mission, making good on his word and sucking my tongue hard. My hand trails up to his hair and I tug at the roots, drawing a groan from him. The feel of his tongue against mine is devastating. When Enzo shifts, his cock presses against my stomach. I'm all too aware of it.

His hands run down my curves before gripping my hips. He turns around in a move that has me pressed against the wall. When he breaks our kiss, I let out a noise of protest that is quieted when his lips follow a path down my throat. I buck under him, trying to push myself closer to his length.

I feel Enzo smile against the swell of my breasts. When he manages to free one of them, he doesn't hesitate to close his mouth over a hard bud. I whimper softly.

"Keep making sounds like that, sweetheart," Enzo murmurs. "I'm begging you. Unless you want me to go easy on you."

When he looks at me, his eyes are filled with desire and something else that I can't figure out. His thumb moves over one nipple, teasing and pinching until I start to writhe.

"Tell me what you want me to do," he says softly as he continues to squeeze my nipples, moving from one tit to the other. "Do you want me to kiss you until those pink lips are swollen?"

His thumb drifting up and tracing my bottom lip. My heart pounds so hard I'm afraid he can hear it.

"Or do you want me to sink my teeth into these sexy dark nubs? Mark you there until it's clear you're mine?"

I moan in reply when he punctuates the sentence with a sharp tug on my nipple. My eyes nearly roll back into my head when he leans down to suck the sting away.

"How about I go further down?" Enzo's tone is deceptively gentle, warm like butter, a contrast to the filthy things he's saying to me. His hand trails down my legs to the open slit in my dress. It's easy for him to shift the material away, his hand inching toward my core. "How wet are you, *principessa?*"

"Enzo," I gasp when he rubs his finger against the dampness of my panties.

Heat erupts inside me when he shifts my panties to the side before thrusting one finger deep inside me.

"Fuck," he swears softly, awe in his voice. "You're soaked, Rosa."

His voice is so full of lust it threatens to drive me crazy. I roll my hips, pressing down against his finger, which is still inside me. I moan softly, scraping my nails along his arms.

He lifts me up, and I immediately wrap my legs around his waist. His muscular body holds me up without any effort. He walks us to the bed and drops me down. My breasts bounce from the impact. His heavy heated gaze threatens to set me on fire.

"Take it off," he commands.

The zipper of the dress is on the side so I'm able to pull it down. I sit up on the bed and it falls away. My red lacy bra comes next. With each article of clothing removed, Enzo's expression grows tighter. He looks like a man on the verge of losing control, which is exactly what I want. When my panties come off, I look at him, my legs already shaking in anticipation.

"Now what?"

"Lie down," he says.

I do so, feeling my cheeks heat. I never imagined I would be here, spread eagle on my bed while Enzo Russo watches me like I'm the only thing that exists. His eyes meet mine.

"I can't get over how perfect you are," he tells me.

He groans low in his throat, climbing onto the bed and

settling between my legs. Placing a hand on each side of me, he leans in and kisses me hard. His hand moves downward, toward my clit, and I writhe under him when he starts to tease the sensitive bundle of nerves. I can already feel the looming orgasm.

Enzo pulls away and shoots me a smirk before shifting and dropping back between my legs. He doesn't hesitate to dip his head and lick me from entrance to clit.

"Enzo," I cry, overwhelmed with emotion.

He growls softly and my heart skips a beat. I grip his hair, hard enough to hurt, but he doesn't seem to mind. He pushes his tongue inside me, eliciting various sounds from me that aren't entirely words. My spine practically arches off the bed when he continues to thrust his tongue inside me.

"Do you want me to make you come, sweetheart?" Enzo asks against my pussy lips.

I moan, too far gone to reply. I yelp when his teeth scrape against my clit.

"Yes," I say on a whimper when he adds a finger to the mix. "Please, please, make me come."

I feel him smile against me as he continues. One hand trails up to my breast and he squeezes once. I rest my hand over his and my heart practically melts when he locks our fingers together. Sparks burn hotter beneath my eyelids. And then, suddenly, the pressure explodes.

I scream, gratefully that Enzo chose bedrooms for us that are separated from anyone else's in the house. My eyes flutter shut as I struggle to catch my breath. A languid sensation pulls on my muscles. When I open my eyes, they immediately connect with Enzo, who has moved up. He's staring at me, his gaze filled with something so soft, yet possessive, it nearly takes my breath away.

I smile softly, sitting up and pushing him onto his back.

His eyes gleam when I climb over him. Very slowly, I work his buttons open. Enzo's perfectly still, content to watch. I manage to take off his shirt, leaving his top half bare. When I lean down to kiss him, he responds, kissing me back with as much passion and raw fire.

I break the kiss to suck on his neck, kissing my way down his chest. I pause halfway down, my eyes landing on the scar on his chest. My hand reaches up to trace it. I can't help but wonder who hurt him like this.

"Don't ask," Enzo warns, his eyes growing hard.

I ignore him. "What happened?"

"Rosa…"

For some reason, I've chosen this moment to try to coax him out of his shell. It's admittedly bad timing.

"Please, just tell me? Who hurt you?"

He grows cold so fast it gives me whiplash. Enzo sits up, shifting away from me. He runs a hand through his hair and looks at me for a second before getting up.

"I can't tell you."

"You can't or you don't want to?" I ask, tears pricking the back of my eyelids.

Still, I don't cry. I can practically see the internal war raging within him. It would hurt him if he saw my tears, but I'm angry that we can't seem to bridge this gap.

"I can't say it, *principessa*. At least, not to you," he says, his voice hollow.

"I understand," I say tonelessly.

"Fuck," I hear him say under his breath.

I don't look at him as he walks out of the room. but my heart does break a little. And I realize with a start that I care much more than I thought I did. Which is made even clearer when I stand and pick up his shirt that lays discarded on the floor of my bedroom. I pull it on, buttoning it up to my chest before sinking back into my bed. Then I look up at my amazing masterpiece on the wall.

I fall asleep like that, surrounded by the scent of him. My last thought before I fall asleep is that Enzo Russo could ruin me.

CHAPTER 13

Enzo

We haven't spoken in two weeks.

I've barely seen her, thanks to some problems that have been arising with the businesses abroad. I've been busy trying to fix them, and Rosa seemed content not to approach me. She's been busy with wedding preparations. And now, the day has come and I'm seated in a pew at the church, behind Rosa's mother and some other family members.

Beside me are the D'Angelos, Carlo and Christian with their respective spouses. Rosa's standing to the side of the aisle, radiant in her bridesmaid's dress. She hasn't looked at me. Not once. Standing in front of her is the maid of honor, Kiara Coleman.

On the opposite side is the groom and his two grooms-men. Roman looks great in his custom-made tuxedo, although there's a hint of nerves in his expression, which I find amusing. His eyes alternate between staring at the closed doors leading into the church and his daughter, who's in her grandmother's arms in front.

After a few more minutes of waiting, soft slow music

starts to play signaling the bride's entrance. Elena walks in on her father's arm, and I hear a tiny gasp from Daniella D'Angelo.

"She looks so beautiful," the redhead whispers.

"Yeah she does," her sister-in-law Astoria agrees.

The bride glides down the aisle to the front. Her father hands her over to the groom and the ceremony commences. I only half-listen, too distracted by the sight of Rosa in front. Then it gets to the vows and I concentrate on what the couple says.

Elena goes first. "Rome, I've known you since I was a little girl with stars in my eyes. I knew you when those stars dimmed and I knew you even when I didn't believe in stars at all. Through every moment of my journey, you've been there. Sometimes, I didn't even realize it. Sometimes, I really despised you."

That draws a laugh from the guests.

"But through it all, my heart has always known you were the one for me. We hit a big iceberg when I lied to you and took something of yours away. But I'm going to make this promise to you today that it'll never happen again. By marrying you, I'm yours now and forever, in sickness and in health and all that."

Another laugh.

"I love you so much, Roman De Luca. And I'll say it to you every day, through every fight. You've shown me your heart and I'll do my best to protect it. Always and forever."

By the time she's done, there's more than one teary eye in the crowd. When I look at Rosa, she's crying, too. A little subtly. I smile even as my heart aches at the sight.

Roman says his vows and it's equally romantic. When they're pronounced husband and wife, Rosa finally looks at me, and my heart races. I know exactly what she's thinking.

This is going to be us in a few months. But I don't think she'll be able to walk down the aisle if our relationship remains in the state it currently is.

I've always been great at fixing things. And fixing us might be the most important thing I ever do.

The wedding ceremony ends and we move to the reception—a lot of loud music, dancing, guests having fun. I stay in a corner with some of the men. Rosa approaches me once and places a kiss on my cheek, a kiss that feels more perfunctory than anything else. And then she goes back to the bride's side. My eyes are fixed on her from across the room as she talks to her friends.

"I know that look," someone says beside me, drawing me from my thoughts.

My eyebrow lifts as I turn to Christian D'Angelo. "What look?"

"The look of a man that's fucked because he's starting to realize just how much he cares."

"Really?" I drawl. "And how would you know that?"

The man smirks before throwing back a shot of vodka.

"Listen, man, I don't usually give out advice like this. I'm sure you'll work shit out eventually, but be careful not to take too long. Some things are out of our power, and sometimes we risk hurting those we love the most."

"Noted," I say dryly, although I do take his advice to heart. "And exactly why are you in such a good mood?"

"It's a wedding." Christian shrugs. "It reminds me of my own."

Love really does weird things to people. But who am I to question it?

"Since you're in such a good mood," I state, "I need a favor."

His brother's right by his side, but I've quickly understood that Carlo D'Angelo doesn't talk much and only speaks when absolutely necessary.

"I'm listening," Christian says.

"I need you to help me find someone," I inform him, hating that I have to give this information away. But I've been searching for a year and I've gotten no results. The D'Angelos are well connected and they have contacts in the city that could be highly beneficial. "A man in his late forties, probably works or used to work as a hired assassin. Red hair, and the right side of his face has been badly burned."

"Name?" Christian asks.

I shake my head. "No idea, all I have are details of his description. And he's extremely proficient with a knife."

He looks at his brother, who shrugs, but I can tell there's a hint of recognition in their eyes.

"We'll have to get back to you on that," Christian states.

"Thanks. What do you want in return?"

He inclines his head with a small smile. "Don't worry, Russo. Not everything has to be a deal. I'll help you find him out of the goodness of my heart."

"And here I thought all made men had hearts as black as their souls."

"Some of us found a way to keep both our hearts and souls intact," Carlo murmurs.

Conversation shifts to another topic until Tony Legan approaches us with a frown on his face.

"Hey, could you help me check something out with the CCTV?" he asks Christian.

"What?"

"Mikey says he saw some strange woman lurking around. Looked Russian."

My eyebrows rise. "Let me guess, blonde hair, long legs?"

His gaze cuts sharply to me. "You know her?"

"Not exactly. But I'm pretty sure she's a Mincetti."

All three men stiffen.

"What would a Mincetti be doing at my sister's wedding?" Tony asks, brown eyes flashing.

"My best guess is that they're looking for trouble," I reply.

"They never do anything without good reason," Christian mutters. "Every action is deliberate when it comes to them. How the hell did you meet her?"

"She approached me," I say on a shrug. "They seem to have a vendetta against the De Lucas and me by association. I'm not sure what it is. I kept quiet because they didn't seem to make any moves after our meeting."

"What did they want?" Tony questions.

"They wanted me to choose. Between a partnership with your family and theirs. I chose yours."

I watch as that information sinks in.

"It still doesn't explain what they want," Carlo states.

"Yes, but we're going to find out," Christian says, a determined look in his eyes. "Let's go, Tony. First we need to confirm if she's actually a Mincetti. This is good, actually; I've been curious about that family for years."

He and Tony walk away just as the women arrive. Christian kisses his wife on the cheek and tells her he'll be back. Rosa moves over to me. I don't hesitate to wrap my arms around her waist.

"Hey," I greet.

She offers me a warm smile that confuses me slightly "Do you want to dance?"

"Sure, sweetheart."

I lead her to where the married couple glides across the dance floor. Rosa and I start to sway, and I arch an eyebrow at the smile on her face.

"You're in a good mood."

"It's a wedding, Enzo."

"So everyone keeps saying. I'm unsure why an event has any power over a person's emotions."

She shakes her head. "You're so annoying."

"Pretty sure you mean amazing," I tease.

Rosa rolls her eyes. "I've been thinking, though. And I feel like I owe you an apology."

That gives me pause. "About?"

"The other night. I never should have pushed you like that. You asked me to stop and I should have listened."

My hand tightens around her waist. "Don't apologize for that," I say sharply.

I should be the one apologizing. Because I know deep down that I'm the problem here. She's trying her hardest to bridge the gap, but I can't help the things I've been hardwired to feel since I was a little boy. I keep wanting to break free of the shackles, but it's even harder because I know with her, there's no going back.

"We were in the middle of something and I ruined it," she says, her eyes soft.

After I left her room, I went to mine and took a cold shower while feeling completely miserable. My entire life, I've had to be strong and emotionless. Rosa is challenging everything I've become and it's making me a little insane. The worst fucking part is, I don't mind. "You didn't ruin anything, sweetheart. I promise."

"I talked to my mom about it and asked for her advice. She told me to be patient. To accept who you are and what you're ready to give me."

"What about wanting better?" Something hard thuds in my chest.

She lets out a soft sigh. "Maybe that is my better."

My hand tightens around her waist. "No, I don't accept that."

"Enzo…" she says sadly.

"No. I'll tell you everything. Whatever it is you want to know. Because you're mine, Rosa. And it doesn't matter what it is, as long as I get to make you happy. That's all I want, *principessa*. I'm going to make it right. I swear."

When she looks at me, there's an openness to her expression, and she nods once in understanding. My heart thuds as I lean down to kiss her. Her lips mold with mine perfectly, like they were made to do that. She was made to be mine. And I'll be damned if I ever let her go.

WHEN WE GET HOME, I tell her everything. About my parents' death. How someone broke into our house.

"It happened in a manner of minutes. The assassin snuck up on us. We were the only ones in the house and we were having dinner. I remember us smiling, we were happy. Until we noticed someone in the room. My dad barely had any time to bring out his gun before his throat was slashed." I swallow softly.

Rosa's seated on the bed, staring at me, her eyes twin pools of heartache. I'm leaning against the wall, trying to look anywhere but at her. I asked her to give me some space while I told her the truth. I couldn't bear to feel her hands on me while I relive the worst day of my life.

"My mom screamed for me to run. I couldn't, though; I was petrified. It wasn't until he threw a knife at my mom's chest and her screams grew quiet that I remembered to move. I jumped out of my chair and moved toward her. At that point, the guards outside had been alerted that something was wrong, and they were almost there. The assassin only had time to slash me across my chest before running. I was bleeding out, too. I probably would have died, but I was rushed to the E.R. and survived."

Her eyes are glassy, but she blinks and they clear somewhat. Very slowly, she gets off the bed. Her steps are cautious. She wraps her arms around my waist as soon as she reaches me.

My lips curl into a small smile. "It happened about two decades ago. It's alright. But it's played a lot in who I've become and why. I may come across as a dick sometimes but if there ever was a reason to change, it'd be you Rosa."

She shakes her head against my chest. "There's nothing alright about what happened to you," she mumbles.

I let her hug me for a few more seconds before she pulls away. She looks up at me, and I can tell she wants to say something but she hesitates.

"At least now I understand why you're so fucked up," she says with a soft smile.

As soon as she says it, it's clear why I'm so drawn to her. Because she could have chosen to say anything. She could have said she was sorry, but instead, she made a joke. Which is infinitely better.

I run my hand through my hair. "You have no idea what you're talking about, *principessa*."

She continues to smile, and I'm so glad this is going so well.

"Your parents would have been proud of you," Rosa says, her expression growing serious.

"Sometimes, I'm not so sure about that," I murmur.

"Try not to be so hard on yourself." Rosa's hand reaches up to my jaw. My skin tingles where she touches. "You're marrying a woman you don't even know to protect your father's legacy. As crazy as it sounds, I think you're a good Don, a good leader. You're trying to take care of your family."

I smile bitterly. "I'm sure they wouldn't agree. And you have no idea how I've lived my life until now, sweetheart. I didn't always make the right decisions."

"Yeah, but yesterday is gone, right? Never too late to do better. You're trying to make things right now, and for some crazy reason, you chose me," she counters. "That's all that matters. Now and in the future. We'll work through everything together."

Her expression is so earnest and insistent I have to smile. "That's if you don't kill me first," I say.

"Or if you don't kill me," she retorts

When she shifts closer, I place a kiss in her hair. "I would die a thousand deaths before I ever hurt you," I say, not realizing until after the words are spoken that I should have kept that to myself.

She stills for a moment, gazing into my eye, and I know that she knows it's true, which can't be good.

What the fuck did I just do?

"Did you ever catch him?" Rosa asks after a few minutes have passed. "The man who murdered them?"

Anger immediately flares through me, hot and fierce. "No," I grit out. "He escaped. I've never found him."

"I'M SORRY, ENZO."

Not as sorry as he's going to be when I find him. And not as sorry as whoever helped him infiltrate our home is going to be. I know the assassin had to have had help. He couldn't have gotten in and he certainly couldn't have gotten out without it. I have to know what really happened.

All that's been driving me the past few years is revenge. It's one of the reasons I came back to New York. I could have stayed away. For a while, I was more than content to let my uncles lead. I didn't give a fuck about anything. But when you see someone's eyes in your nightmares as often as I do, when their face haunts your every moment, there's no other choice but to look for them. To try to end it all.

But I'm terrified that I waited too long. And now all I've got to chase after are ghosts.

CHAPTER 14

Rosa

As soon as my eyes open the next morning, I immediately seek out warmth that should be beside me on the bed. Enzo and I fell asleep soon after our conversation yesterday. Or at least, I fell asleep. The last thing I remember is him stroking my hair as he watched me. Blue eyes, a dark, possessive gleam in his expression.

I yawn softly before sitting up. Enzo's not anywhere in sight. Cool air slides in through the open window. I'm a little upset that he didn't stick around to wake up with me, especially since it's only a few minutes after six. There's nowhere he needs to be this early. The door to the closet is open, so I climb off the bed, walking in that direction.

When I open the door, Enzo's there, the brightness of his phone in his hand illuminating his face. He looks up as soon as I appear in the doorway. A light smile touches his lips.

"Hey," I say softly. "Why are you up so early?"

"I always wake up early," he replies.

It's only one simple sentence. But now that I have context for what happened to him, that sentence sounds like so much more. I can't help but wonder how he was able to cope after what happened to him. Did he seek out therapy? Then I try to imagine a guy like Enzo sitting on a couch talking to some bespectacled man or woman. I doubt it. He's too arrogant to believe anyone could help him work out his demons. He wouldn't even talk to me about it, despite how hard I pushed. I'm still surprised he actually did.

His cool gaze lands on my exposed thighs before drifting up to my face.

"You have never looked more beautiful than you do now, *principessa*," he tells me.

I flush, my heart growing ridiculously warm. I probably look awful, my hair a rat's nest and my face devoid of makeup. But I'm wearing one of his shirts, and knowing him, I'm sure that's what he's alluding to.

"So," I say awkwardly, "what are your plans for today?"

Enzo drops his phone on the table in the middle of the room. He walks toward me, light, controlled steps. I swallow softly when I realize he's shirtless, in only boxer briefs. Is that how he slept last night? I can't remember.

He reaches me and brushes a thumb against my cheek. "I was thinking we could spend the day together. Maybe hang out in bed or go out somewhere, it's up to you. What do you think?"

"Sounds scandalous," I say with a shiver. "And lazy."

He smiles and places a soft kiss on my lips.

The press of his lips against mine hits me with such intensity, my entire body tingles. I bring my palm up to his shoulders, pulling him closer as he slides his tongue inside my mouth. A moan travels up in my throat. My fingers curl and I hold him even tighter.

Enzo's hand slides up to my neck. He holds me there, the touch feather-light but also possessive. Every slide of his tongue against mine sends a tremble through me. I can feel the wet glide between my legs acutely. His other hand slides over my hips to the curve of my ass. When he squeezes hard and makes a low growl in the back of his throat, my body practically melts against his.

I pant softly as he ends the kiss to nip a line down my neck, pulling the skin between his teeth, lightly sucking. His fingers glide up my leg, drawing my dress upward and giving him a glance at my panties. Heat tugs in my lower stomach. Enzo rubs the damp material of my panties up and down, causing me to break out in shivers.

"Always so wet for me," he murmurs in a dark voice.

There's nothing I want more in this moment than him. I slide my hand down his body, cupping his erection. He draws in a rough breath between his teeth before dropping his gaze as I slide my hand from his base to his tip through the material of his boxers.

"You have no idea how much I've thought about this, Rosa," he whispers.

I look up at him. "Living up to your expectations?"

"Nothing could ever compare," he growls and kisses me hard.

I gasp into his mouth and he swallows it, consuming me. Enzo picks me up without breaking our kiss. One minute we're in the closet, the next we're in the bed. I'm still on top of him, his back against the headboard as he practically devours me.

"You want me," Enzo says against my lips, his breaths mingling.

It isn't a question, but I know he wants a response. So I nod.

"I want you," I breathe.

His hand kneads my ass before he slaps it once, the sound echoing in the bedroom. A growl of satisfaction emanates from him when I lean down and place soft kisses on his neck. It's thrilling, having this much access to him. My hands glide over the planes of his chest. All those hours in the gym really pay off.

Grabbing my hips, Enzo pulls me closer to sit on his erection. I grow even wetter when he grinds me against his cock. A heated glance meets my eyes and he shifts me slightly to reach down. One finger shifts my panties to the side while two others glide across my clit. Hot pressure expands within me and I arch my back when he slides two fingers inside me. I moan, gripping his shoulders, unable to do anything but rock my hips against his hand.

"You're mine, Rosa." He says the words in Italian. I'm not sure he even realizes it.

I'm too far gone in the throes of passion to say anything. Pleasure licks at my veins, building until it's all I know. When Enzo adds another finger, stars fly behind my eyelids. Needing something to ground myself to reality, I look into his eyes. Which is a mistake. They're so dark, with lust, desire, and another soft emotion I can't name.

When Enzo suddenly stops fingering me, my eyes widen. The pleasure building within me crashes, filling me with desperation.

"No," I cry, trying to grind against him, to keep his fingers in place.

It's no use, though. He abruptly pulls them away, his eyes gleaming.

"You don't get to come until I'm inside of you," he says. He places one of his fingers against my lips, his words light and commanding. "Suck."

A bolt of lust shoots through me. I feel like I'm about to combust from the anticipation, the nerves, the need for him to be inside of me. Still, I slide my lips open, letting him place his finger in my mouth. I close my mouth around it and suck, tasting the sweet tanginess of my arousal. When Enzo tries to slide his finger out, I refuse, my mouth stretching into a smile as I hold it closed.

His eyes gleam in a way that promises retribution.

"Let go, Rosa. Before I fill your mouth with my cock instead of my finger."

The promise sends a shiver through me and I can't help but wonder how he tastes. How it would feel to slide his cock inside my mouth. Enzo groans like he can read my thoughts.

"Not today," he insists. "Today, all I want is to be buried inside of you."

Before I can blink, he's fisting the material of my panties. He rips the lace with barely any effort, baring me to him. He runs a thumb over my wet pussy. The touch is almost reverent, and when he looks at me, there's something vulnerable in his eyes.

"If I fuck you, Rosa, there's no going back."

"I know," I whisper.

He kisses me then, slipping his tongue into my mouth. Kissing him feels like taking a hit of a drug, one you can't stop using because it's so addictive. He manages to work the shirt I'm wearing over my head, leaving me completely naked. I shift on his cock, slowly rocking my hips and grinding against him. When he captures a nipple in his mouth, a shaky breath escapes me. My hand goes up to his hair, gripping it tighter as he sucks my nipple hard before switching to the next one. My eyes threaten to roll back into my head, my pulse throbbing between my legs.

"Enzo," I moan, unable to take it anymore, desperate for release.

I manage to work him out of his briefs, pulling out his cock. For a second, I just stare at it. He's so hot and heavy in my hand. I pump him in my fist, just once, causing him to let out a hiss. I'm about to stroke him once again when he grabs my wrist, stopping me.

A look passes between us before he lifts my hips and slowly lowers me down onto his cock. Enzo groans, and I gasp, my breath catching. Tears prick my eyes from the burning sensation of him stretching me. I haven't even taken him in entirely yet, but I already feel so full.

Enzo grips my hips. I'm not sure which one of us is trembling. The look of hunger in his eyes sends a fresh wave of warmth up my spine. My nails dig into his shoulders as his hand traces down to my clit. He rubs it in a circular motion and I moan, feeling a hot buzz. After a minute or two passes, I meet his gaze, my eyes telling him that I'm ready.

"Are you sure, *principessa*?" he asks.

"I'm sure," I breathe.

He hesitates before slowly guiding me down until I've taken him in. Every single inch.

"Fuck," Enzo says through gritted teeth.

He grips my hips hard enough to bruise as every muscle in his body pulls tight. I'm trembling and my eyes burn as his heartbeat races against mine. I press my face into his neck, trying to deal with the onslaught of emotion.

"Rosa," Enzo says, his voice teetering on the edge of control, "baby, I need you to move."

His words set me into motion. I move slowly, rocking my hips in a circular motion and grinding my clit against him. His hands move all over me, from my ass to my spine. He grabs fistfuls of my hair, kissing me hard as he slaps my ass. A tingling sensation spreads through my body as I shift from grinding against him to rising and taking him in. The pace is slow and Enzo seems content to let me set the rhythm. My breasts bounce as he slides in and out of me until suddenly it all becomes too much.

I'm shoved off the edge, my body shuddering as I scream his name. His mouth latches onto mine, drawing a shaky breath from me. When I come, he's watching me intently.

"I want to hear you scream my name like that forever," he whispers softly, nipping at my earlobe.

His gaze threatens to light me on fire. When he's sure I've calmed from the orgasm, he grips my hips again, pulling us closer together. He shifts me up and down, bouncing me on his erection, hard. My moans tremble in my throat. My fingers splay against the headboard behind his head as I try to ground myself.

I scream repeatedly as he continues to thrust up, jackhammering into me.

He fucks me like it's a marathon, and the only thing on both of our minds is getting to the end. When I come the second time, I fall onto his chest, unable to keep my eyes open. Enzo comes too, shuddering against me as he finishes inside of me. He presses a kiss against my shoulder.

I'm still underneath him, boneless and full of contentment. My hands curl in his hair, unwilling to let go. Our heavy breaths fill the silence.

"There was never anything better than you, *principessa*," Enzo says after a few minutes have passed and I start to breathe normally.

My heart warms. I try to climb off him, but his grip tightens, keeping me there. He's still inside me and I'm pretty sure his cock is still slightly hard. I smile against his chest.

"Enzo, I need to get up."

"You promised to stay in bed with me all day," he retorts.

"And I will. As soon as I take a shower," I tell him, already feeling wetness trickling down my thighs.

"Fine." He sighs, nipping at my lips. "We'll take one together."

A laugh escapes me as he carries me in the direction of the bathroom. We spend at least an hour in there, taking time to get to know each other's bodies. When we return to his bed, I'm exhausted. Enzo calls for his butler to bring us breakfast in bed.

He keeps his promise. We spend the rest of the day talking and fucking. He doesn't look at his phone once.

Late in the evening, we're lying side by side on his bed. I'm tracing circles across his chest, and my heart feels full. I haven't been this happy in a very long time.

"Why don't you have any tattoos?" I question.

My brother has a chest full of them. Tony has a few, even Michael. It feels a little odd that he has none.

"I've never felt the need to get one," Enzo tells me with a small smirk. "Plus, I don't like the feeling of a needle piercing my skin."

My lips curl into a smile. "Oh my god, you're scared of needles."

His eyes narrow. "How did you come to that conclusion? I'm not scared, baby. Just… cautious," he mutters.

I snort. "You're definitely scared. That's amazing. I swear," I say, still laughing.

"Keep saying I'm scared, Rosa. I dare you," he says.

"You're scared," I return boldly.

The air tenses for a second. He climbs over me, his eyes simmering with heat as they trail over my body. I expect him to kiss me but instead a mischievous look passes across his face and he starts to tickle my sides. My eyes bulge as I erupt in a fit of giggles.

"Enzo," I say between laughs, trying to shake him off. "Stop."

"Not until you take it back, baby," he says, his hands continuing their assault.

"Okay, okay," I say, still giggling. "I take it back."

He finally pauses, letting me catch my breath.

"You're a big, bad wolf. You don't get scared," I tell him with a grin.

"Good to see we're on the same page," he says, leaning down and capturing my lips in a sweet kiss that leaves me breathless.

When he pulls back, the lopsided grin on his face causes my heart to stutter. His genuine smiles are so rare it makes me want to bottle each one up and keep them forever. I want every day to be like this for the rest of our lives.

The thought of the rest of our lives is sobering. We need to have an important conversation.

Enzo falls back onto the bed and I lay my head on his chest.

"So I was thinking," I start, "we're meant to get married before the end of the year, right?"

Enzo makes a sound of agreement.

"Well, the first step to achieving that is choosing a date. We don't have a lot of time anymore."

"What day do you want us to get married, *principessa*?"

I look up at him. "You want me to choose?"

He nods. "I don't care what day it happens. All that matters is making you my wife."

My chest grows warm and a feeling of excitement over-comes me. I sit up to look at him.

"Well, I was thinking a Christmas wedding," I announce. "Christmas has always been special to me. It's pretty cheesy, but I used to fantasize about getting married on Christmas Day. There would be snow and bright lights everywhere. It would be amazing."

It isn't until I'm done talking that I realize how still he is.

"Enzo?" I ask, confused.

A muscle ticks in his jaw and his expression shutters. In a flash, the warm, easy look he has been giving me all day vanishes. In its place is a coldness I thought I would never have to see again.

"No."

Just one word. I don't even know what he's saying no to yet, but I feel my heart crack.

"No what?" I ask as he climbs off the bed and runs a hand through his hair in agitation.

"No, we're not getting married on Christmas. Pick another date, Rosa," he tells me.

It's more like a command, his tone leaving no room for argument. Something chilly slides down my spine.

"You just said you didn't care what day it is."

"We can get married any other day but that one, *principessa*."

My jaw tightens and I feel myself start to grow angry. "Why not?"

When he doesn't reply, my emotions flare.

"I don't want to fight about this, Rosa."

"Well, too bad," I say, getting to my feet as well. I pull on one of his shirts that was discarded on the floor and stare him down. "You don't get to say things and just expect me to obey without a second thought. I'm not a robot and I can't read your fucking mind! Tell me why, Enzo. Now."

He opens his mouth to speak, then hesitates. His lips clamp shut and he looks away. I let out a scoff.

"Unbelievable," I mutter.

I'm about to yell at him, maybe call him an asshole, when there's a knock at the door. His eyes meet mine briefly before he moves towards it. I sit on the bed, my chest still tight. I can only see Jason's blonde hair as Enzo stands in the doorway.

"What?" Enzo questions, a bite to his tone.

"We've got a problem. A really big one. The Mincettis. They killed some of our men, burned down one of our warehouses in Russia. Things are pretty tense over there."

I don't miss the way Enzo stiffens. I stay put on the bed. The Mincettis are one of the mafia families, but no one really knows who they are. Jason says something else to Enzo, but his voice is too low for me to discern what. A few seconds later, he steps back and Enzo shuts the door. He looks back at me, jaw tense and eyes brimming with barely controlled rage.

"Baby, I need to go," he says, his voice surprisingly soft.

I arch an eyebrow. "What happened with the Mincettis? What relations do you have with them?"

His jaw ticks. "They made me a deal, asked me to partner up with their family instead of yours. I refused."

"They asked you to marry one of their daughters instead," I say in understanding.

"Something like that."

"And now?"

"They want revenge, I guess. The details are murky; all I know is that they've stirred up some shit I need to fix."

"Are you going to war?" I question, feeling my heart thud in my chest.

He shakes his head. "Even if I wanted to, I couldn't. We don't have the resources for that. And I never start a fight I can't win."

"Roman would help you," I suggest.

"He would. But I'm not interested in a fight. I don't think the Mincettis are either. They've done their worst, and I expect them to slink back into the shadows now."

"So where are you going?"

He holds my gaze as he replies, "Russia."

My heart rate quickens. The Bratva, which is the Russian mafia, and the Italian mafia don't exactly get along. The closest they've come to it was when a Russian woman married an Italian Don, which led to the Mincettis. Still, Italians who bravely decide to go to Russia famously return without their heads.

"Don't worry, *principessa*. I won't die," Enzo says with a soft smile. "It might take a while before I get back, though."

He places a hand on my cheek and I lean into his touch. "How long?"

"I don't know, weeks. It's a volatile situation over there. But I need to regain control."

"Okay. Do whatever you have to do," I say, my mind trailing back to our argument.

He must see it on my face because he sighs, taking a seat in front of me. "Rosa, I don't want the last thing we do before I leave to be arguing."

"We technically didn't argue. I made a suggestion and you shut me down without a good reason."

"I'm sorry," he says, his tone sincere. "I would do anything for you. Just not that."

I sniff and look away, but not before I see shadows flicker in his eyes. "You have important things to do, Enzo," I remind him.

"Baby…"

"I'll be right here when you get back," I say to appease him.

He places a hand under my jaw, lifting my head up so I'm looking into his eyes. "You're mine," he says fiercely.

"I know," I say on a sigh.

When he captures my lips with his, I let him. I let myself feel everything, even the heartache. It's too much. I always feel too much when it comes to him. I hate that thirty minutes ago, we were so happy, and now that's all gone.

Enzo's packed and ready to go in a matter of minutes. I get dressed as well and follow him downstairs. Something painful thuds in my chest when I watch him say goodbye to his cousins. Maria even gives him a hug. I can't help but wonder if he wants kids. I'm on birth control, but it's a pretty important conversation we probably should have had before he fucked me without a condom.

After saying his goodbyes to his cousins, he kisses me once more on my forehead, and then he's gone. My heart feels empty almost immediately.

"Already whoring yourself out to your future husband I see," Isabella says to me.

I look at her with a raised eyebrow. She gestures at my neck and my hand goes up to touch the hickey I'm sure must be on display. *Fucking hell, Enzo.*

Although, really, was I expecting to have sex with Enzo Russo without him marking me in some way?

"That makes no sense, Isa," I mutter with a small smile. "I can't whore myself out to my future husband."

I've learned that the best way to deal with Isabella Russo is to kill her with kindness. She's not a bad person, just hurt. According to Jason, who was all too willing to provide me with information, Isabella's never really gotten over Enzo leaving her when they were teens. They were close as kids. Which is how I know she'll forgive him. Eventually. And maybe that forgiveness will extend to me, eventually.

Enzo calls regularly, so I can hear his voice. So I can at least confirm he's alive. And I pick up, sometimes. But other than that, I've turned to pottery. I once told Enzo that I only do it when I have to release a heavy weight in my chest, emotions I can't handle.

And with his absence, that's exactly what's happened. My brothers, Elena, everyone's notices something's wrong. Especially when I turn up at the house every day and immediately escape into my pottery room. Roman thinks it's because I miss Enzo, and I don't have the heart to tell him that's wrong.

Because I do miss him, with every fiber of my being. But I'm also worried that when he comes back, all our progress will be lost and we'll ultimately have to start all over from scratch.

My eyes latch onto the glittering ring on my finger. It's proof. Proof how much he cares. Because even before he knew me well, he was willing to give me a ring belonging to his mother. Enzo might like to pretend he's all ice and jagged lines, but I've seen evidence of his heart within.

I might unequivocally be his. But he's mine, as well.

CHAPTER 15

Enzo

The Russians are fucking bastards.

It takes six weeks to clean up the mess caused by the Mincettis while also ensuring that my businesses don't implode. I have to give it to them, they're thorough when it comes to revenge. Not only did they burn my warehouses, they took control of some of my drug fields in Russia. Meaning I had to negotiate with Russian thugs and convince them to return those fields while making sure relations didn't turn hostile.

But now all that is done, and I'm returning home. I used to despise New York and everything it stood for. The Russo mansion never really felt like home to me, especially not after what happened within its walls. But that's all changed. Because I know there's someone there waiting for me. Olive skin, blue eyes. I missed Rosa. So much that sometimes, it was fucking hard to breathe. I wanted nothing more than to come back home and pull her into my arms, but I couldn't break my concentration. Absence makes the heart grow fonder. And now my heart physically can't bear to be away from her anymore.

Now, nothing will keep me away from her. Unfortunately, I hit my first roadblock when I arrive and Isabella's not there. Matthew and Maria rush over as soon as they see me with wide grins. It's odd. A year ago, I scared the hell out of them, and now both of them are welcoming me with a hug. I'm surprised to find I don't mind. I like it, even. In a very short time, I've come to care a great deal about my little cousins.

I ruffle Matthew's hair after we're done exchanging pleasantries. "Where's Rosa, Mattie?"

He smiles. "She's at her other house."

I arch an eyebrow. "Her other house?"

Maria nods enthusiastically. "She took me there. To her art studio. And she's teaching me to potter, *cugino* Enzo. She says I have a natural talent. And we paint sometimes, too."

"She plays video games with me," Matthew chimes in.

I chuckle softly. Although unease slides through my chest at the fact that Rosa has turned back to her art again. I can only hope it's because she wanted to teach Maria. Judging by how infrequently she wanted to talk to me over the phone while I was away, however, I doubt it. Something's still wrong.

"You two go back to watching TV. I'll go and get Rosa," I tell them. I turn around, then pause, realizing something. "Where's your mother?"

The twins exchange a look, something passing across their eyes before they look back at me. Their expressions are guilty.

"She left," Maria answers.

My jaw clenches. "She left when?"

No one should be able to leave this house without me knowing.

"Three days ago. She said she was going on a trip," she

replies nervously. "Told us not to tell. Isa said we shouldn't tell either."

Denise leaving the house secretly is extremely worrisome for a plethora of reasons. I'm guessing she's feeling better. The woman has never liked me, which means she could be plotting something. My hand trails over my jaw.

"Don't worry. I won't do anything to her," I tell the twins to ease the concern in their eyes.

"You promise?" Matthew asks shakily.

I nod once. They offer me small smiles before returning to the living room. I only take a moment to get changed into something else before I'm heading back into the car and driving to the De Lucas'. I'm granted entrance through the gate, although once I step through the foyer, Roman's waiting for me. A glass of some liquid in his hand.

An eyebrow is raised as I approach.

"Well, if it isn't a man who dared to step foot in Russia and survived," he says, tipping his glass in acknowledgment.

Despite myself, I smile. "Not everyone's a coward, Rome."

"Ehh." He shrugs, apparently not offended by the insult. "The only reason you survived is because your family hasn't had as many skirmishes with the Russians in the past. If I stepped foot in their territory, I'd be shot in a manner of seconds. That's why we don't mix. Not worth the risk," he says, shaking his head.

"I can imagine," I say dryly. "Where's my wife?"

Roman's expression grows amused at my tone. "Funny you call her that when you're not even married yet."

"We're married in all the ways that matter," I return.

I know it in my heart. Rosa and I might not have walked down the aisle yet, but she's mine. She promised.

"That's interesting. Just one question, did you do something to her when you left on your trip?" Dark blue eyes trail over my face. "Because my sister's a talented artist, but I get worried when she spends such a long time locked up in that room of hers. What did you do, Russo?"

"I'll let you know when I'm ready to start talking to you about private matters between me and her."

His eyes darken. I remember he's still her brother, and we'll be family soon, so I ease up.

"We're fine," I say, hoping it's not a lie. "Just a couple issues to work through. You know how it is."

I can see in his eyes that he understands. "Fine," Roman relents. "Just be careful with her. She's my only sister, Enzo."

"I know."

"She's upstairs in her studio. Third door on the right," he tells me, gesturing with his hand. "Oh, and the two of you are expected at our Thanksgiving dinner in a couple of weeks. I believe congratulations are in order since your wedding will follow soon after."

I grit my teeth and nod, too focused on reaching Rosa to think about what he means by that.

There's no reply when I knock on the door. After knocking one more time, I enter, and the sight of Rosa takes my breath away. She's at her work station, seated with her hands around some clay as she molds. There's a soft, serene smile on her face. She's wearing ear buds, which is why she doesn't immediately react to my presence.

I should be taking in the room, the various art pieces, ones in incomplete states, the ones she has finished. But I only have eyes for her. I continue to study her for a few seconds and come to two realizations. The first is that she's the most beautiful right here in her element. She looks like a goddess.

The second thing I realize is that I love her. I love her, and the world doesn't shatter. Nothing crashes around me. Everything's perfectly still as my heart beats with the knowledge. Rosa's eyes finally lift, blue eyes fixed on mine. They widen with surprise before narrowing just as fast.

Her movements are slow as she takes out her earbuds and gets to her feet. She walks toward me.

"You could have told me you were coming back," she breathes, expression slightly hesitant.

I need to touch her more than I need air. "Are you going to hug me or not, baby?"

"I would, but I'm pretty dirty," she says, gesturing at the apron covering her dress and her hands.

"I don't care, *principessa.*"

Her expression softens and she lets out a sigh. In the next breath, she's throwing herself into my arms. I hold her to me, surprised when a slight tremor ebbs through my hand. It tightens in her hair as I hold her even closer.

"Fuck, I missed you, sweetheart."

"I missed you too," she whispers. "Despite the fact that you're the world's greatest asshole."

That makes me chuckle. And then she lets out a soft laugh of her own and it feels like Heaven. Being in her arms feels like Heaven.

WE'RE IN MY BED, which Rosa confessed to sleeping in every night since I left. If I didn't love her already, the confession would have definitely been my tipping point. We're lying on the bed, still fully clothed as she tells me how she has spent the past few weeks.

"I already picked out my wedding dress," she informs me. "I'm having it custom made by an Italian designer."

"Yes, Roman mentioned to me that the wedding is a few

weeks after Thanksgiving," I say, fishing. I'm a little worried she went ahead without the Christmas wedding, despite my hang-ups about it.

"I decided on a date without you," she announces. "I figured since you didn't 'care,' I was allowed to. Don't worry, it's not on Christmas. I'll be spending that day with my family since you seem to hate it so much."

My eyes narrow. "I'm your family."

"Yes," she nods, "and it'll be official on the twenty-eighth. A few days after Christmas. Does that please you?"

"I'm not feeling particularly pleased with the sass in your tone," I mutter.

She rolls her eyes. "Dickhead."

I pull her closer. "Keep saying things like that and it'll be really hard for you to work tomorrow, baby."

"Good," she whispers. "You've got a lot of making up to do. Six weeks' worth."

I smile, running my hand through her hair. "I'm sorry I can't give you a Christmas wedding."

"That's okay, babe," she murmurs. "I had a long time to work through my issues about that. I might have accidentally drawn you with my boot in your cheek to relieve some of my anger," she says with a grin. "But I'm okay now."

Dry amusement fills me. "Can I see the drawing?"

She shakes her head. "No one's seeing it. Ever. I did make a few vases and ceramic sculptures you'll like. Dany has an art gallery showing coming up, and she's trying to convince me to put some of my recent works up for auction."

"Do you want to?"

"We'll see if they sell."

I'd buy every last piece of her art to keep her happy.

"Tell me about you, though. How was Russia?"

My lips curl into a smile as I give her a recap of everything that went down, making sure to soften the more bloody parts of the story.

"And Jason? I haven't seen him?"

"He's still back there. Taking care of the last few issues."

"He'll be okay, right?" Rosa questions worriedly.

I nod. "Don't worry, *principessa*. Jason will be back soon." I look at her. "Now that we've both got all our questions out of the way, can I have my kiss?"

She grins. "You can have as many as you want. But tomorrow, we have to talk about wedding preparations. There's so much to do, Enzo. You wouldn't believe it."

"Sure, no problem," I murmur. I'll say anything to get her to slide those pink lips against mine.

When she leans closer, I don't hesitate. Her lips are soft, her tongue hot and wet. When she sighs into my mouth, violent lust roars through my blood, dulling my vision. She has no idea the effect she has on me. How deeply she has imprinted herself onto me.

THE WEEKS GO BY FAST. Rosa and I settle into a real relationship, our wedding looming closer with each passing day. My eyes open as I feel the sheets rustle and her warmth sliding out of my arms. We were up late last night as I went all out in trying to make up for the past few weeks.

"Where are you going?" I ask as she gets out of bed and stretches.

"Church," she informs me. "I'm trying to go more regularly. Mom has been on my ass about it."

"No," I groan, pulling her back into bed. "If you're so intent on going to church, how about you get on the bed while I say a prayer between your legs?"

My voice is low and husky as I whisper into her ears. I don't miss the way she shivers.

Her lips twitch but she doesn't smile, hitting my shoulder instead. "You're disgusting. But I have to go, babe. How about you come with me?"

My eyebrow flicks up. "I doubt I'm wanted in a church. What if I burst into flames?" I question.

Rosa smiles, amused. "I'm sure that won't happen. Come on, it'll be fun."

"When has mass ever been fun?" I grumble.

I genuinely couldn't remember the last time I went to church. Maybe when I was little and I didn't have a choice but to go with my uncles and their families.

"Good point," Rosa concedes. "But we're going. We'll even take the twins and Isa, if she's interested. Most of my family will be there, too. Come on, let's go."

I groan when she flashes those beautiful blue eyes at me. I really am screwed when it comes to her. Because less than an hour later, I'm walking through the doors of a church with my arms around Rosa's waist. The twins are with us, too.

The service is already underway when we arrive, and more than a few people turn to stare at us as we walk toward the front where the De Lucas are seated. I'm surprised when I see some D'Angelos as well. Specifically Christian and his wife, with two little kids I'm guessing are theirs.

We settle into the pews for the mass. I practically count down the minutes until it's done.

After the service, Rosa moves to talk to Elena, and I drift outside where the men are standing. I caught Christian's gaze during the service. He has something to say to me.

Tony's talking when I arrive, and Christian's expression is blank as he listens. Roman's jaw is tight.

"You want me to investigate your father?" Christian questions.

"No," Tony says. There's something vulnerable in his expression. "I want you to find my mother. I had Michael look into it a few weeks ago. According to my father, she left the country years ago, but there's no record of her leaving. Mikey checked. He tried to find her but he couldn't."

"Why the sudden interest in finding her?"

"That's for me to know," Tony returns. "Can you find her?"

"Tony, just let it go," Roman says, his expression hard.

"Fuck off, Rome."

Christian offers a short nod. "I'll look into it," he tells Tony.

"Really?" I drawl. "Because I asked you to look into something for me. And you haven't gotten back to me."

His jaw tightens. "I found your guy weeks ago. I just wasn't sure how to tell you."

"Tell me what?" I ask, feeling my heart speed up.

His eyes meet mine. "We should probably go somewhere more private to talk."

"I'll ask Rosa to take the kids home," I say in agreement.

After saying goodbye to them, I get into Christian D'Angelo's car and direct him to one of the clubs I own. I'm tense the entire ride. There are Christmas decorations going up, which further worsens my mood. The thought of the holiday hasn't started to evoke violent thoughts from me. Yet.

The club is quiet considering it's still during the day. Jason's there, getting things ready. He arches an eyebrow as Christian and I pass. I shake my head to tell him there's no trouble, and he goes back to what he's doing while I lead Christian into my office.

"Alright, I'm listening," I say once we're settled. "Where the hell is the bastard?"

Christian leans forward. "I knew who he was. When you described him, my brother and I realized he seemed similar to a man our dad used to do business with when we were younger. His name is Trent Cane, but in the underworld, he's known as the Butcher."

"Fitting," I say dryly, wishing he'd get to the point.

"The Butcher's pretty infamous. He was responsible for a dozens of murders two decades ago. If you wanted someone dead without the death being traced back to you, the Butcher was your guy. He never wore a mask, never hid his face, but he was pretty good at disappearing. He's not American, and I'm pretty sure Trent Cane isn't his actual name. He's also not registered, which is why he's been able to keep his real identity a secret for such a long time. He disappeared fully about ten years ago, going underground. I guess he got older, too slow to continue working."

"I don't give a fuck how old he is. I just want to know where the hell he is," I bite out.

"He's dead," Christian says.

His voice is clear, concise, straight to the point. I feel my heart stop as the air around me stills.

"What?" My voice comes out gravelly.

"He died a couple of years ago, Enzo. A heart attack. I'm sorry, you're too late."

I don't move muscle as I take in his words. The look in Christian's eyes is sympathetic, maybe verging on pity. I can't focus on that, though. Rage billows through me, hot and fierce. I thought I knew anger. But it's nothing compared to how I feel right now.

"He's dead," I repeat tonelessly as the words finally sink in.

I start to understand the implication. I'll never have my revenge. I really was too late. All this time, and I was just chasing after ghosts.

I rise and in a moment, I'm pushing off the contents of the desk. Everything goes crashing down, including my phone. My skin feels hot and my heart pounds too fast. I need to hit someone; I need to kill someone. I can't kill Christian, though. That would be messy.

He's completely calm, taking in my outburst with a blank expression. "You can still find the person who hired him," he offers.

"I know exactly who it is," I growl. I'm about to say something else when Jason bursts through the door, eyes wide.

"We've got a problem," he informs me. "Denise is back."

Fucking hell.

CHAPTER 16

Rosa

"Can we have chocolate milk on Thanksgiving?" Matthew asks from the back seat of the car.

"Of course, sweetie. You can have as much as you want. There'll be lots of food, too. My mom used to cook but since we're expecting lots of people this year, we'll have to cater the meal. I'm sure it'll be delicious, though."

"And there'll be lots of other kids," Maria says excitedly. "Like Cat. I like Cat."

Cat is Daniella and Christian's daughter. Her full name's Catherine, and she's an adorable little girl who looks just like her mother.

"I'm sure she likes you, too. And yes, there'll be lot of kids. Christmas will probably be the same. I can't wait," I say with a grin.

"You want to see Santa, too?" Maria asks, wide-eyed.

"Sure, I want to see Santa. But Christmas is more than just gifts from Santa, my darlings. You get to spend time with family and there's lots of food and snow!" I sigh happily. "I used to love playing in the snow with my brother when we were little. It was the only time we were ever really close. We would make snowmen and snow angels."

"We like snow angels," the twins chorus.

"Yeah," I say, feeling nostalgic. "You'll get to make all the snow angels you want this year. I can't wait for Christmas."

I might not be getting my dream wedding, but I'm also not letting Enzo's grumpy ass keep me from enjoying a day I genuinely love. Especially since he won't tell me why.

"You said the gifts don't matter, Aunt Rosa," Matthew says tentatively. "But we're still getting gifts, right?"

I laugh. "You'll get as many gifts as you desire," I promise. "And after Christmas, we'll have my wedding. We're in for lots of excitement the next couple of weeks."

The twins grow quiet as we drive up to the house. As soon as we walk through the doors, they run to their bedroom. I move into the living room, taking off my jacket and getting ready to settle down and maybe watch some TV. I briefly wonder what Enzo had to discuss with Christian that was so important. That man and his secrets.

I'm barely on the couch for more than a minute before something goes wrong.

"Marie!" I hear Matthew shout.

I rush out of the living room and find them outside in the hallway. Maria's collapsed against the wall, brown eyes wide as she clutches her throat. Matthew's crying in front of her, trying to coax his sister back.

"Oh god!" I gasp, rushing over and crouching in front of her. "Maria! What happened, baby? Talk to me."

She continues taking short, gasping breaths. Her throat starts to swell and her face starts to redden. Something clicks in my head.

"Allergy," I breathe. She has a peanut allergy. I search her pockets. "Matthew, did you eat anything at church?"

He nods just as my hand closes around a wrapper in her pockets.

"We just ate the candy Daniel gave us. Maria told me not to tell you. She only had one bite. Daniel said his mom got it for him. I-I didn't know." He starts crying again.

"Isa!" I scream.

She comes running a few seconds later, eyes wide.

"Her EpiPen," I say, my heart thudding in my chest.

Isabella doesn't waste a second before stumbling into the twins' bedroom. She reappears quickly holding a small metal box. I lean away as she brings it out. Her steps are practiced, precise. She's done this before.

Isabella kneels carefully in front of the little girl. She lifts the pen in the air and quickly injects it into Maria's thigh.

We wait for a minute or two until Maria manages to take a full breath. When she does, I fall back on my ass and take a rough, shaky breath.

"Oh god. Thank you, thank you," I cry.

"We need to call 911," Isa murmurs.

I cradle Maria in my arms while Isa gets up to grab her phone. "You're okay, darling. It's okay," I say softly, kissing her forehead.

The whole thing probably happened in less than five minutes, but it feels like an eternity has passed. I'm still running my hand through her dark hair when I hear the sound of a gun being loaded. I turn around and my eyes widen when I see Denise standing there.

Dark brown eyes are fixed on me, full of fear and hate.

"Step away from my daughter," she orders, pointing her gun at me.

Panic lodges in my throat. "No, Denise. She's fine. She ate some peanuts and had an allergic reaction. But Isa already used the EpiPen. She's going to be okay," I assure the woman quickly.

The look in her eyes doesn't let up. It's almost unhinged. "I said get up!" she shouts.

"Mama," Matthew cries, walking toward her. But I don't trust the look in Denise's eyes right now.

Very carefully, I get to my feet. "Stay behind me, Matt. Stay with your sister."

I hear Isabella's footsteps as she reappears. She takes in the scene silently before speaking up.

"Denise," she drawls. "You're back." Her voice is measured, controlled.

"She was trying to harm Marie," Denise accuses.

"Maria had an accident, Denise. Put the gun away. You're scaring the children," Isabella states.

Instead of letting go, Denise's hands tighten around the grip of the firearm.

"I told you, Isa. I told you he would ruin us. He brought this bitch into our family and now she's trying to kill my daughter."

I make sure not to make any sudden moves. "I would never hurt Maria, Denise. I swear."

"Mama," Matthew tries again, voice low and full of fear. "Aunt Rosa didn't do anything."

"Keep quiet, Matty," his mother says without looking at him. Her eyes never leave my face as she continues to aim at my chest.

I swallow softly. "We need to get Maria to the hospital," I say, hoping she'll see sense. This is her daughter we're talking about.

Isabella's trying to talk her down when Enzo arrives. The look on his face is more furious than ever as he walks toward us. His eyes meet mine, and I see so many emotions pass across his face. Anger's the most prominent one, but I also see fear. Fear for me.

"What the fuck is going on here?" he asks.

Jason is at his back, jaw clenched as he takes everything in.

Denise whirls around, changing the direction of her aim. For the first time, I see her expression flicker. Nerves, fear. At least that means she hasn't completely lost it.

"Stay back!" Denise yells.

Enzo's lips curl in distaste. "You're not going to shoot me," he says confidently. His eyes meet mine. "You okay, baby?"

I nod. "We need to get Maria to a hospital."

Enzo lets out a breath. "Jason, go pick her up."

Denise doesn't move as Jason walks over to the little girl on the floor. I'm glad she's still conscious, although she looks very weak, her brown eyes blinking slowly. "Isa, go to the hospital with Matt. Jase will drive you."

Isabella hesitates, her eyes drifting to Denise.

Enzo's jaw ticks. "I wasn't asking, Isa."

"Don't kill her, please," she begs, rushing off with Matthew before he has a chance to run toward his mother.

I sigh in relief once they disappear through the front door. At least Maria will be okay. Some of the men guarding the house have drifted inside, looking for what's causing trouble. Enzo tells them to leave, until it's only the three of us left. Me, Enzo, and Denise. Who is still pointing a gun at him. Seriously, her arms have to be hurting by now.

"Aren't you getting tired of holding that up?" Enzo asks dryly. Despite myself, I can't help a small smile. Great minds think alike. "Drop the gun, Denise."

She doesn't. Enzo's jaw tightens.

"You disappear for weeks and return only to hold someone at gunpoint in front of your kids," he says angrily. "Mother of the year."

Denise finally speaks up. "Do you want to know where I was?"

"Isabella mentioned that you went on a trip to clear your head. I confirmed you were still in the U.S. and I stopped caring after that."

"You should care," Denise says, her voice nearly hysterical. "You should really care. I was looking for him."

Who?

Enzo's eyes narrow slightly. Like he knows exactly who she's talking about.

"He's dead, though," Denise mutters. "It's really such a shame. I was looking to give him a job. Can you guess what?"

I have no idea what they're talking about and it's pissing me off.

"You know," Enzo says, and his voice sounds so cold a chill runs through me.

"Of course I know." Denise laughs. "It might have happened long before I married Leo, but his brother's wife told me. You remember her, right? She passed away from cancer. But in her last months, she told me everything. How your uncles conspired to have their brother killed. They hired someone to do it. Someone who would do a clean job, murder all of you. But you didn't die," Denise says sadly.

My hand flies up to my mouth and I suddenly feel sick. Enzo doesn't look at me. I swallow the cry that threatens to escape my throat. Sorrow fills me. I can't even begin to imagine how he must be feeling. But when I really study his expression, there's not even a flicker of surprise.

"You knew," Denise says, confirming my thoughts.

"Of course I fucking knew," Enzo grits out. "No one else would have benefitted from my father's death apart from his brothers. I got confirmation when I was seventeen. After I heard them gloating about it. They were always fucking fools."

"Y-y-you never d-did anything," Denise stutters.

"I didn't," Enzo agrees. "I could have. After I heard them laughing and making fun of my father, I could have killed them both. I had so many chances to kill them. And a part of me wanted to. You have no idea how much I'm regretting not doing it now, Denise," he says, anger coating his words.

"Why didn't you?" Denise questions, her voice low.

"I didn't kill them because while they might have given the order, they weren't the ones who slit my father's throat. They weren't responsible for cutting my mother down. I saved my revenge for the man that actually did the deed. My uncles were inconsequential. Plus, they succeeded. They were idiots, but they did manage to kill my father so I decided to let them live. I wasn't ready to become Don at the time either. They only lived for so long because I saw it fit."

I can't move, I can't breathe. All I can do stare in shock.

"You're sick," Denise mutters.

"I really am. My seventeen-year-old self-rationalized not killing those responsible for my father's death as being unnecessary. But I'm not seventeen years old anymore, and there's literally no reason I should keep you alive. Now tell me, why did you try to contact the Butcher?"

"Leo never trusted you," Denise says shakily. "He always said they shouldn't have kept you alive. That you'd stab them in the back. He said you would kill him. That you would kill all of us."

"I did kill him," Enzo says, sounding bored.

"Yes. And I was terrified. I couldn't eat, I couldn't sleep.

Because I was the only one left and you were the Don. There was nothing I could use against you. I couldn't get my children out of the house. I thought you were going to harm them. I've lived the past two years in fear of you."

"So you went to find the Butcher to see if he could finish the job?"

"Not just you," Denise says. "Her, too. I wanted you both gone."

She gestures at me, which is a big mistake. The mask on Enzo's face falls away, revealing the fury underneath.

"Don't fucking look at her. And you won't fucking touch her," he growls.

"I can't do anything anymore. I couldn't find the Butcher," Denise says, heartache clear in her voice.

My eyes widen when the gun in her hand thuds to the floor. *No, no, don't,* I want to tell her, but the words don't make it past my lips. That's her only defense. I'm growing warier of Enzo's next actions with each passing second.

Denise looks on the verge of collapse.

"He's fucking dead," Enzo spits. "He's dead, and I'll never have my fucking revenge. But maybe killing you will ease some of this fucking pain in my chest."

He pulls out a gun and that pushes me into action. My stomach plummets, an icy sensation moving over me with the realization of what he's about to do.

"No!" I yell, putting myself between him and Denise.

Enzo's eyes are clouded over. But when I reach for his arm, he pauses, drawing a hard gaze to mine.

"Stay out of the way, *principessa.*" His voice is slightly calm, but the edges are rough.

"I can't do that," I say softly, but he's not listening to me.

His jaw is clenched as he looks back at Denise. His hand

tightens around the trigger of the gun and I stand in front of it, blocking Denise.

"Fucking hell, Rosa. Move!" he yells.

"No. She's Maria and Matthew's mom. Their mother, Enzo! They're still your cousins, and they don't deserve to lose their mother," I plead. "More than anyone, you should understand what it's like to grow up without parents."

My chests heaves as I try to force him to look at me. But he keeps his gaze fixed on a point behind me. On her.

"You can't kill her," I say forcibly. "Enzo!"

He finally looks at me, blue eyes filled with so much anger and sorrow it makes my heart ache. I say the words that I know will stop him.

"If you love me, you'll let her live."

I watch as the impact of my words hit him. His jaw clenches before his eyes fall shut.

"Fuck!" Enzo yells, punching the wall hard.

I flinch. He only punches the wall once before inter-locking his arms behind his neck, trying to regain some control. My heart is still thudding in my chest as I watch him. When he finally looks at me, some of the emotion in his eyes has ebbed.

"That was a little dramatic," he says dryly.

"Did it work?" I ask hopefully.

He doesn't reply. He pulls his phone out and sends a text. Two seconds later, two men appear in the foyer.

"Lock her up in a room," he orders, gesturing at Denise with a gun. "No one goes in or out."

Relief nearly cracks my heart in two. "Thank you," I whisper as the men move to do just that.

Denise doesn't even put up a fight as she's led away.

"Don't thank me yet, baby. I have a half a mind to lock her in a mental hospital," he tells me.

A small smile touches my lips. "That might be ideal. She needs help."

He pulls me into his arms and I rest my head against his chest. I can feel his heart racing. He runs his hand down my spine before it settles in my hair. He holds me even closer.

"You have no idea how terrified I was when I saw her pointing that gun at you," Enzo whispers.

"I thought you weren't scared of anything," I mumble, wrapping my arms around his waist.

"I'm scared of one thing," he says. "Losing you."

I swallow softly as those words warm my chest. "And needles," I add with a small smile.

"You're annoying," he mutters, and I laugh. He finally pulls away after a minute or two. "We should probably go to the hospital and check on Maria."

I stare at him for a second. I can't believe that despite everything that's happened, he's worried about her. It's proof of what I've always known. That he has a heart. He might hide it, but he does. I want nothing more than to climb into bed with him, but I'm also worried about Maria and how she is.

We go to the hospital and after confirming that she'll be okay, Enzo drives us back home. As soon as we step through the walls of our bedroom, he says four words to me.

"It happened on Christmas Day."

My heart stalls and my legs fall to a stop. I look up at him for an explanation.

"My parents," he tells me. "They died on Christmas Day. We were having Christmas dinner when they were killed. I remember being so happy one moment because I had gotten exactly what I wanted. And in the next moment, my happiness turned to ash."

He brushes a thumb against my cheek.

"That's why I can't marry you that day, baby. Because it's the worst day of my life," he says softly. "And I should have told you when you asked, but you said you love it so much. And I couldn't bear the thought of saying something that would cast a cloud over your joy. Christmas is yours, *principessa*. I didn't want to take it away from you."

A searing ache cuts a path across my chest.

"I understand," I breathe.

That night, I hold him in our bed as he breaks down and mourns the loss of his parents. He may have lost them twenty years ago, but now the pain is raw and acute, especially since there's no means of escape, no release. There's no one to kill and no one upon whom to exact his revenge.

And I know it's not fair, but a part of me is glad that it's all over. He can stop now. He can stop hiding, shutting his emotions out. I wish I could have realized that revenge was his ultimate goal. Enzo always gave everyone parts of himself because if he couldn't trust his own family members, he couldn't trust anyone. And now that I understand him at his core, I'm going to help him find himself again.

Every single tiny sliver of him, every part. I'll stop at nothing until I put him together. Until the man I've fallen in love with is whole again.

CHAPTER 17

Enzo

Rosa works me from my briefs before wrapping a hand around my hard cock. She starts to stroke me slowly and my jaw tightens. She glances up at me. I've never told her this, but her eyes are a window into her soul. One look and I could probably tell what she's thinking, what she's feeling.

I can see all her love and desire for me in those beautiful blue eyes. My heart beats overtime as she slides her tongue against my shaft.

"Fuck," I hiss. "Rosa."

She smiles up at me, still stroking my cock. "Relax."

She's enjoying this, seeing me on the edge of control. It gets her off. Her other hand moves up my taut abs, ivory fingers painted dark red, soft as velvet. Her gaze meets mine as she licks the head of my cock. I groan softly.

When she sucks in as much of me as she can, my hand moves down to her hair. I hold her there, needing to feel more as she sucks and licks my cock.

"That's it, baby," I say, my voice rough. "Take me in deeper."

Rosa complies, her mouth opening wider as she slides further down, taking in a few more inches. She gags a second later and the heat building in my spine grows hotter. Rosa pulls pack to suck in a ragged breath before trying to take my cock in all the way again.

"Fuck," I growl again, louder this time.

She hums a breathy moan around my shaft and I only have time to tap her cheek in warning before heat erupts inside me so violently my eyes flutter closed. Rosa swallows every last drop of come. Once she ascertains I've got nothing left to give, she rises to her feet, running a hand through her hair, which is a mess.

"Enzo, it took me an hour to do my hair," she says with a pout as she tries to fix it.

"Your hair's always beautiful," I tell her.

"Yeah, right," she says with a small smile

I grab the back of her neck and pull her lips to mine, kissing her deeply and sliding my tongue into her mouth. We kiss for what feels like hours. Once we come up for air, I push her back down onto our bed and settle between her legs to return the favor.

THE DAY PASSES with us lying languidly in bed.

"What should we do tomorrow?" Rosa asks. "I was thinking we watch some movies. There's this new one that came out a couple of months ago and I've heard it's pretty good."

Her movie idea would be nice as hell, if it wasn't for the small tiny fact that tomorrow's Christmas. Rosa's avoided mentioning Christmas like a plague since I told the truth a month ago. It's been pissing me off because she proved me right. I knew she would try to ignore her feelings about the day because of me.

"I was thinking we go for a drive tomorrow morning. There's something I need to show you," I tell her.

"A drive?" she says hesitantly. "I don't really want to go outside."

She means she doesn't want me to see all the Christmas decorations that line practically every corner once we leave our home. It's honestly adorable how hard she's trying.

"We're going. Don't worry, you'll like it. I promise," I tell her.

"Fine," she mutters.

She moves to grab her phone and I watch as she answers a couple of texts, probably about our wedding in a couple of days. Heat washes through me at the thought of what I'm going to do tomorrow. I know in my heart that's it's the right thing. Nothing has ever felt so right.

WHEN I WAKE up the next morning, she's already out of bed. She stands by the window of our bedroom watching the snow fall. I was worried we wouldn't be getting snow today but I'm glad we did. There's a soft smile on her face as she takes it all in. I climb off the bed, moving behind her and wrapping a hand around her waist.

"Why do you like the snow so much?" I ask softly.

"It's pretty," she replies. "And simple, uncomplicated. Just harmless tiny white crystals falling from the sky."

"It's freezing cold, though," I murmur, drawing her closer.

"I like the cold." She smiles.

"I know you do. Come on, go get ready. We leave in thirty minutes."

Rosa turns around to look at me. A curious expression crosses her face. "You're not getting in the shower with me?" she asks.

We've been showering together almost daily the past few weeks. But I know for sure that if I get into a shower with her right now, I won't be able to stop myself from fucking her. And that would not be ideal. Especially not today.

"Nah, I need to do something real quick. I'll shower after you."

"What do you have to do?"

"It's just work stuff, Rosa," I reply, my expression carefully blank.

She's still suspicious, but she nods before heading into the bathroom. I take the time to place a few important calls ensuring everything is in order. We're out of the house in thirty minutes.

She asks me where we're going the entire ride, and I pretend not to notice the way her eyes light up with each exceptionally bright tree we pass.

If I didn't know she loved me, it became pretty when she said no to Christmas dinner at her brothers' place because she didn't want me to be alone. And she wasn't about to make me sit through a dinner celebrating the day my parents passed. She didn't say so to me but to her brother, who made sure to pass it along to me.

The moment I heard that, my plan became finalized in my mind. I did everything in my power to keep her from finding out. And now that the day is here, I can only hope she goes along with it.

When we make the turn leading to her old neighborhood, Rosa looks at me and her eyes narrow.

"What are you doing? I told you I wasn't going to the dinner," she says accusatorially.

I don't answer her immediately, keeping my eyes fixed on the road as we drive up to the De Luca mansion.

"Enzo!" Rosa says icily.

"Patience, *principessa*." I murmur.

She doesn't speak again until we're parked in the driveway of the house. When I look at her, her arms are crossed and there's a stubborn, resolute expression her face.

"Rosa…" I start.

"I'm not getting out of the car and I'm not going in," she says without looking at me. "And even if I wanted to, I'm wearing jeans and a T-shirt. There's nothing festive about my outfit, so you might as well drive me home."

"That's okay. You'll get changed here," I tell her.

"What does that even mean?" she mumbles.

"I mean we're not here for the dinner. The dinner's not happening anymore."

Her gaze cuts to me sharply. "What did you do?"

I smile. "I'm here to drop you off. You need to get dressed, sweetheart."

"Dressed for what? And what do you mean, there's no dinner? Where are the twins? You dropped them off here yesterday morning, right?"

"The twins are probably already at the church with Roman and the other guys."

Her head cocks to the side in confusion. "Enzo, it's Friday."

"I'm aware."

She grits her teeth, blue eyes growing fierce. "Start making sense," she snaps. "What's going on at the church?"

"A wedding," I reply, my heart beating faster. "Ours."

She stiffens, her eyes moving over my face. "Enzo, our wedding's in three days."

"Not anymore, *principessa*. I had it moved up. We're getting married today."

Her mouth drops open. "Are you kidding me?!" she screams when she finally gets over her shock.

I smile and climb out of car to see Elena and a couple of other women, Rosa's friends, standing in the doorway of the house. Some of them are already dressed in the red brides-maid dresses Rosa picked. Elena offers me an encouraging smile as I move to open Rosa's door.

She steps outside, her eyes still disbelieving.

"Enzo, I swear if this is some joke..." Her words trail off when she notices her bridesmaids in front of the door. "Oh god, you're being serious."

"I'm sorry for lying, baby. But I had a chance to give you the wedding of your dreams and I took it."

"But..." She pauses, seemingly at a loss for words.

I feel a little bad so I lean closer and stroke her hair. "I wouldn't have had to resort to this if you hadn't been so adamant about pretending Christmas doesn't exist. You love it. I pulled some strings to make sure we got married today."

"That shouldn't be possible."

"It's possible," I assure her. "Especially since you're the only one that was in the dark about it. Even the twins kept it a secret. I wanted to surprise you."

"I still can't believe this," she mutters.

"We're getting married today, sweetheart," I tell her, almost not believing the words myself. "Nothing could stop me from making you my wife. Nothing except you. If you don't want to, now's your last chance."

Her eyes narrow and her mouth turns down in a frown. "Oh, so you plan a wedding behind my back and decide to give me a choice in the matter, what? An hour before the ceremony?" she asks.

"Two. Enough time to get you ready," I say with a small smile. "And I'm sorry. I'll apologize all you want."

"You'll be apologizing forever," she corrects, muttering other words under her breath. "I can't believe everyone kept this from me."

"They know what it means to you."

She lets out a soft breath. "You can go. I'm sure you have things to do while I get dolled up. Lena and Dany will fill me in on what happened. After I kill them both. Honestly, if anything, the two of them should have had my back. They're my best friends," she sniffs.

"So, you're saying yes?" I ask cautiously.

Rosa smiles, amused. "You didn't even ask me that when we got engaged."

"Will you marry me today or not, Rosa?" I press insistently, needing her to say the words.

"Yes," she says on a sigh. "I'll be there. I promise," she adds, her voice sincere.

She gets on her tiptoes to place a soft kiss on my lips. And after one last smile, she walks over to her friends. A part of me wants to pull her into my arms and never let go, but I force myself to get back in my car and drive away. After today, our fates will be intertwined. Forever.

A PART of me doesn't believe it. Not when I'm fully dressed. Not when I enter the church to pews filled with relatives and loved ones.

I'm nervous as hell as I walk up the aisle. My eyes find Isa and the twins in the front row as I move to take my place in front. Maria and Matthew wave at me, identical grins on their faces. Despite everything, I'm glad Rosa talked me out of killing their mother. I would have regretted it if I had. If only for their sake. Denise is on anti-depression meds now, receiving treatment and slowly returning back to normal.

Jason's behind me, acting as my best man. It feels like fucking déjà vu because a couple of months ago, I was here and Roman was getting married. I almost can't believe I'm the one standing here right now, which is ridiculous because I knew even then that I would marry Rosa. I just didn't know how deeply in love I would be with her when it happened.

My heart beats faster when the song for the bride's entrance starts. Right on time. I brace myself, waiting. The doors open and she finally appears, holding her brother's arm. They both walk down the aisle, and I can't look at much else apart from her. Out of the corner of my eye, I notice her mother crying. I hold my breath until she's standing in front of me.

"Hey, baby," I mouth, taking her hands. "You're the most breathtaking thing I've ever seen."

She's not wearing a veil, so I get to see her beautiful smile.

"I'm still killing you for this," she whispers.

The priest clears his throat and the ceremony starts. I wish I could say I was present for every moment, but it seems I have a bad habit of tuning out wedding sermons. Including mine. I manage to say the right words at the right moments, though. The priest says the customary vows and then it's my turn.

Everyone falls silent as I clear my throat to speak. I'm not addressing them, though, only the woman standing in front of me.

"I have a couple of things to say, Rosa. They're not vows per se, I just wanted to thank you," I say quietly.

Her expression softens. "You're about to make me cry. Aren't you?"

"Probably."

Everyone laughs. I inhale deeply before I begin.

"I lived the majority of my life alone. Without any love, any warmth. And I foolishly thought that was living. I was content to remain that way. I saw no reason for change. Until you came into my life. I'm aware I always say that I know everything, but I really didn't know what I was getting into with you. There was a lot of uncertainty, a lot of nights spent wide awake as I thought about you. There were a lot of fights and arguments, which, trust me, I wasn't expecting," I say dryly.

Rosa lets out a watery laugh, tears already sliding down her cheeks.

"You really turned my life upside-down. In the best way possible. And you made me feel. When I met you, I finally felt warmth, and although the journey was slow, I learned to love, too. You have the best heart, baby. I see it every day. You were ready to give up something you loved because you didn't want me to feel hurt or lonely. Today was the worst day of my life, but now I get to replace that memory with this one. With the sight of you standing in front of me as you agree to marry me. I really don't deserve you, sweetheart. But I'll spend every single waking moment of my life working hard toward being better for you," I promise. "Thank you, Rosario. Thanks for being my bright light. Thanks for pushing me to be better. Thank you for being my better half. I love you."

Once I'm done, the church erupts in cheers.

"I love you, too. So much." Rosa mouths the words to me as tears continue running down her face.

Once the shouts from the guests lesson, we're pronounced husband and wife.

"You may now kiss the bride."

The touch of my lips against hers is searing. I feel it deep within me. She's mine, and I'm never letting go. We walk down the aisle together—Mr. and Mrs. Enzo Russo. I don't let go of her hand once as we head over to the reception.

The look on Rosa's face as she takes in the venue is worth everything I did, going behind her back. The decorations are in Christmas colors, red and green. There are bright lights everywhere and a giant Christmas tree to the side. It's exactly what she wanted.

"You're the best," she says in awe.

I smile. "Merry Christmas, *principessa.*"

"Merry Christmas, *mi amore.*"

The rest of the night is spent in the company of the family I've gained thanks to her. Looking back at my life, I never would have thought I would be here. But Rosa made it possible.

I want to share every aspect of life with her—both the joys and sorrows, embracing all facets of her love. I envision growing old together, raising children, and cherishing her eternally.

"What do you say I put a baby in you tonight?" I suggest. She grins, "Can we start in the car?" Excitement courses through me as I eagerly carry her to the car, my anticipation fueling an intense passion.

Time to create our legacy.

The End.

Did you like this book? Then you'll love …

Secret Baby for the Merciless Don: A Dark Mafia Romance

A forbidden night with my brother's best friend led to a secret baby for the merciless don.

I wanted out of the mafia world, so I moved away to start a new life.

A funeral forced me to return home, where I found myself in the arms of my sworn enemy, Roman De Luca.

He's as ruthless as he is handsome, and with the passing of his father, he is now the mafia boss.

One night, a fire ignited between us, and I was reminded of why he was my childhood crush.

Disregarding our mutual hate, his new mob boss status, and most importantly, the fact that he's my brother's best friend... we crossed a line that he demands we NEVER cross again.

But as life would have it... I'm pregnant.

READ Secret Baby for the Merciless Don NOW!
https://www.amazon.com/dp/B0CQCGYX1V

Printed in Great Britain
by Amazon